JORDAN'S BRANCH

OTHER NOVELS BY HOWARD OWEN

Littlejohn
Fat Lightning
Answers to Lucky
The Measured Man
Harry and Ruth
The Rail
Turn Signal
Rock of Ages
The Reckoning
Annie's Bones

WILLIE BLACK SERIES

Oregon Hill
The Philadelphia Quarry
Parker Field
The Bottom
Grace
The Devil's Triangle
Scuffletown
Evergreen
Belle Isle

A WILLIE BLACK MYSTERY

JORDAN'S BRANCH

HOWARD OWEN

THE PERMANENT PRESS
Sag Harbor, NY 11963

For information, address:
The Permanent Press
4170 Noyac Road
Sag Harbor, NY 11963
www.thepermanentpress.com

Library of Congress Cataloging-in-Publication Data

Owen, Howard, author.
Jordan's branch / Howard Owen.
1. Preview edition.
Sag Harbor, NY: The Permanent Press, [2021]
Series: Willie Black mysteries; 10
ISBN 978-1-57962-643-3 (hardcover)
ISBN 978-1-57962-644-0 (ebook)

PS3565.W552 J67 2021
813'.54—dc23 2020049223

Printed in the United States of America

To Karen

CHAPTER ONE

Monday, September 2, 2019

Stick is deader than a doornail. Not much doubt about that. From the smell, he's been that way for a couple of days at least.

Other than the fact that I am the local rag's night cops reporter, what has me somewhat interested in his demise is the fact that he owes me money—fifty thousand dollars, to be exact. Well, that's not quite right. He did give me 5K up front.

Still it's a loss. And I guess somebody somewhere will miss Stick too.

I knew something was wrong when I rang the doorbell and then, getting no answer, tried the door, which opened. I almost called the cops at that point, but fools rush in.

It was personal, from what I can see. The shot to the chest and one to the head should have done the trick. The other five or six just seem like piling on. Not much chance of salvaging that faux-Persian carpet. And there are what appear to be cigarette burns on his face. Somebody wanted Stick to feel the pain.

The first wave of cops just arrived, wailing up Patterson Avenue and turning on to Glenburnie and then to Stokes Lane like there was something here more urgent than the corpse of which I informed them via 911 maybe ten minutes ago.

The first ones in the door have their weapons drawn. I am very careful not to reach for a Camel, scratch my balls, or do anything else that involves lowering my arms below straight-up vertical. Still, they put me on the ground. They don't cuff me, but they are deaf to my attempts to explain that I'm only the bearer of bad news, not the creator of it.

"Do you think I would have called you to tell you I just killed somebody and then wait here for you?" I ask.

"Shut the fuck up," a white, bullet-headed bouncer-cop advises.

It's about half an hour before the chief, Larry Doby Jones himself, arrives, no doubt mildly irritated at being dragged from a Labor Day picnic to a homicide scene.

"Here's trouble," he mutters, apparently referring to me instead of the other body on Stick Davis's living-room floor, the one that isn't moving.

The chief sighs.

After he walks around the crime scene for a minute or two, he reluctantly tells his boys to let me up.

"What are you doing here?" he asks. It seems like a fair question. L.D. seems to take offense at the way I always appear to "poke my nosy ass" into what he considers to be police business but which, from where I live, is part of the job of a diligent professional journalist.

He doesn't like it much when I'm at the homicide scene not long after his minions have descended on it. Being the one to actually find the body probably seems to the chief to be stepping over the line.

I explain my relationship with Stick Davis.

"He wanted you to write his life story?"

"Something like that. Do you mind if I smoke?"

L.D. shrugs.

"I don't suppose Mr. Davis is going to mind too much."

I tell the chief and his detective what I know. I was supposed to meet Stick at the Continental yesterday morning, where we were going to go over the draft of the latest chapter of his would-be autobiography and see if he wanted any changes.

When he didn't show up, I wasn't overly concerned. Stick Davis has a long history of not showing up when he's supposed to.

But then he didn't answer my calls yesterday afternoon and evening. So this morning, I drove out here to Westwood to see what the story was.

"And you found him like this?"

I promise L.D. that I haven't touched Stick's body or anything around it.

We're about two blocks inside the city line, in a neighborhood most folks don't know much about. There are a couple of other Westwoods around Richmond, but this one has some resonance for me.

The late Philomena Slade once schooled me on it, expressing shock that I didn't know more about the struggles of "my people." Since I'm an Anglo-African American, Westwood is kind of the story of half my people crapping on the other half.

It was started by freed slaves after the Civil War. There used to be a creek running through it, Jordan's Branch, but that's now buried under the Willow Lawn Drive median. The place was annexed during World War II. It took the city several years after that to get around to providing water and sewer service, and civic-minded individuals in adjoining white communities did their level best to have it razed for a park nobody wanted or needed.

Even the editorial pages of my paper, famous for afflicting the afflicted, fulminated against that idea.

And so Westwood survives, although in a diminished state. The old church that was its centerpiece is still there, but businesses and a post office have chewed away at it.

It is, by Richmond standards, a peaceful little pocket these days, as much white as black. I seldom have had to visit it to report on a dirt nap.

So Stick's violent demise is not just a loss to him but also a stain on a part of Richmond that usually encounters such activity by seeing it breathlessly reported on the evening news. A few of our residents still read my version of the carnage in the next day's newspaper.

"You're not going anywhere, are you, Willie?" the detective asks. I am offended that this pup, about half my age, is using my first name.

"What's it to you?" I inquire.

The chief steps in.

"We got a very dead man here. You seem to have been the last one to see him alive last Thursday. From what you say, he owed you some money. Do the math, Willie."

I have known L.D. since we were teenagers, playing ball against each other. The fact that he would consider me a suspect in what is obviously a homicide kind of stuns me.

"L.D. . . ." I begin.

"You might want to get a lawyer," my old acquaintance says before he and his smirking detective turn and walk out.

"Don't go anywhere," the pup says. I give him the finger. He seems to want to continue the discussion, but the chief grabs him by the elbow and escorts him into the next room.

I am in the odd but not unprecedented position of reporting on myself. How do I write, under my byline, that "Willie Black, a local reporter, found the body"?

There seems to be one, rather unappetizing solution.

I go to the contacts page on my iPhone.

"Hello, Leighton," I say when she answers. "I think I have a story for you."

* * *

Leighton Byrd, one of the two young reporters our penurious chain has let us hire in the past year and a half to make up for six it laid off, is here in twenty minutes. She is wearing a T-shirt emblazoned with the words, "Drink Up Bitches." It comes halfway down to her knees.

"Pool party," she explains.

I apologize for spoiling her holiday fun.

"Are you shittin' me?" she replies. "When you told me what happened, I damn near forgot the T-shirt."

That would have been a pity, I observe. Leighton, who is six years younger than my daughter, does justice to the shirt and no doubt the swimwear underneath it.

I don't intend to permanently cede my byline on this story, even if it was me who found the body. It would be wise, though, to let Leighton break the story.

"So this guy, you were writing his autobiography, and somebody killed him before you could finish?"

She asks me what he was paying. When I tell her, she whistles.

"Wow, he was going to pay you more than I'll make all year, working my ass off fifty hours a week."

"Welcome to print journalism," I tell her, looking about for an ashtray.

The cops are still hanging around, waiting for the medical examiner. Leighton manages to get a few words from the chief, who seems to give preferential treatment to attractive young women in pool-party attire. He does me the kindness of not mentioning to her that I seem to be his prime suspect, although she probably can figure that out for herself.

Then she interviews me, one of the weirder experiences I've had in my ink-stained life. I realize how the interviewee feels, certain that my words will be mangled or misinterpreted.

"Hey, my eyes are up here," she says when I glance down at her notepad. Then she laughs. "Don't worry, Willie. I took shorthand in high school. I won't misquote you."

We leave just as the TV trucks start rolling up the tight little street. This will give some otherwise quiet holiday newscasts a caffeine jolt. I get the hell out of there before the kids who got stuck with weekend duty at the local stations start shoving cameras in my face.

I can handle being a nominal homicide suspect and having to forfeit a hell of a breaking story, but being scooped by the good-hair people would be too much to bear.

"Be sure to post it, now," I tell Leighton when I walk around to her car.

She has the laptop between her lovely knees.

"Already on it," she assures me.

* * *

I'M HOME by one thirty, in time to take Cindy to a swim party of our own, at the Philadelphia Quarry. The text message I sent her was short on details. She wants to know more than "Stick dead. Waiting for cops."

I tell her the story. She knows I've been spending a lot of my spare time the past few months working on Stick Davis's life story. The promise of a big payday salved the pain of not getting to spend more quality time with me.

"So he was just lying there, like dead on the floor?"

I explain that he was indeed deceased and had been for some time.

"Did he bleed a lot?"

"What?"

My right ear's not been the same since part of it was shot off last year when I got a little too close to a story.

"Bleed. Did he bleed a lot?"

"Fuck, I guess so. I mean, that carpet's never going to be the same."

"That's a shame," my beloved says. "Was it a good carpet?"

CHAPTER TWO

Tuesday, September 3

Willow Oaks Country Club is a little outside my comfort zone. Country clubs in general haven't played a big role in my life. However, we're bidding adieu to one of the old guard today, and respects must be paid.

I walk into the entrance nearest where we parked.

"Flemish bond," Cindy whispers, as if she's passing on a state secret.

I don't know Flemish bond from James Bond. Cindy sighs and points to the brickwork.

I stub out my cigarette on the walkway because the woman just inside the door looks like she might Tase me if I don't.

Inside, there's a sign, "Prescott party," at the entrance of a room big enough for two hundred or so people, looking out on a golf course and the James River that floods it every once in a while. I am heartened to see that a bar has been set up. I start to head in that direction. Cindy grabs my arm and says, "Later."

Walter Prescott was my first city editor. He is currently dead, which is the excuse for the party. There'll be a burial later, but they won't have an open bar at Hollywood Cemetery. This is the "celebration of his life." It's a shame Pressy couldn't be here to help us celebrate, but that's the way it goes.

The obit said he was eighty-nine. I've got to hand it to him. He did not go gently. He was on the treadmill at the Y downtown and either through operator error or machine malfunction, the damn thing went from casual stroll to 100-meter dash and threw Pressy all the way into the glass wall facing Franklin Street.

"Never knew what hit him," Bootie Carmichael said when he relayed the sad news to me last Friday. If my long-suffering lungs and liver carry me to eighty-nine and the reaper ambushes me when I'm not looking, I can live, or die, with that.

Pressy was a bastard to work for. He was already past fifty when I started at the paper, and he took great pride in pointing out my literary shortcomings in a voice loud enough to inform half the newsroom.

"Black!" he'd yell. I'd come over to take my beating.

"Where the hell did you learn English?" he might ask. "Is it your second language?"

And then he would point out the vast difference between "presently" and "at present," or how "enormousness" and "enormity" were two entirely different concepts.

Why did I love the old hard-drinking son of a bitch then? I guess because he taught me more in six months than I'd learned in all my college journalism courses. And he raised the bar so high that, when you did something praiseworthy and he acknowledged it, you felt your life had not been completely misspent.

"Not bad," he would mutter, so low that no one but you and he could hear it.

And he actually seemed to worry about me. When he retired, now damn near a quarter of a century ago, he told me that I would go far "if your dick and your smart mouth don't do you in."

I'd already run through a couple of marriages by then, and I guess he knew it was only a matter of time before my lack of reverence for authority would bite me in the ass.

After I was demoted to night cops for refusing to do a sneak interview with a guy dying of AIDS, he phoned me.

"Dammit, Willie," he said. "What'd I tell you?"

"Would you have sent me to ambush that guy?" I asked him when I'd given him the full account of what I was ordered to do.

I heard him sigh.

"Times have changed, Willie," he said. "Change or die."

Well, unlike Pressy, I'm not dead yet. The night police beat might suck on occasion, but it is above ground.

All the old crowd is here at the celebration. Newer folk like Mal Wheelwright and Sarah Goodnight, the two top guns in the newsroom, are present as well. Our publisher, the inestimable Benson Stine, had a previous engagement.

We manage to get seats near the back, close to the bar.

Things go well enough, for a while. A family member and a friend from his church say what you should say about the dead.

But then I see a familiar face and body stand and teeter toward the microphone.

"Damn," I mutter, mostly under my breath. "Jimbo Frisque."

"Who?" Cindy whispers.

"I'll tell you later, after you tell me about Flemish bond."

I hear a few murmurs around me from other now-retired colleagues.

Jimbo was the state editor when I arrived on the scene. He and Pressy had a hate-hate relationship. It probably went back to some slight that happened before my time, but it was exacerbated by the fact that many stories could fall into the bailiwick of either the state or city staff, and any time there was a question of ownership, the two of them went at it like pit bulls at feeding time. It probably didn't help that both of them kept fifths in their desk drawers.

I saw them actually exchange blows once, when a small-plane crash up near the Henrico-Hanover was near the boundary between city and state territory. It wasn't much of a fight, but Jimbo did lose a perfectly good necktie. Newsrooms were livelier back then, although when I tell these stories to the young'uns today, they don't seem to feel the charm.

"So nobody did anything, like fire them or something?" Sarah asked me when she heard the story.

It was a lot harder to get fired back then, I explain.

I suppose some well-meaning member of Pressy's small family thought it would be a good idea to ask the only other living retired editor from his heyday to say a few words.

It wasn't.

Jimbo Frisque, who is pushing ninety hard, starts out on the right note. He mentions the time Pressy and a team of his reporters almost won a Pulitzer Prize. He praises his many years at the paper.

But then the paean turns into a roast.

"Pressy would have been even better," he says, "if he had gone a little easier on the Jim Beam."

A little nervous laughter rises up from the audience.

And then, after a couple of vignettes illustrating Pressy's fondness for demon alcohol, he really steps in it.

Jimbo grins with his store-bought choppers and plunges on.

"And Walter Prescott was quite the ladies' man," he said. "Who can ever forget the Marshall Plan?"

"Oh, God," I moan, as do others.

Cindy just looks at me.

And then Jimbo goes on to give the audience, those too young to have been there, the sordid details of the newsroom's arrangement with a homeowner on Marshall Street.

Nobody knew how it began, but a handful of newsroom guys had an understanding with a man who lived there and who was willing to rent his place out during the daytime, while he was at work. The only caveat was that whoever possessed the sacred extra key and brought his honey there had to be out before five. The whole thing fell apart before I got there, something I will explain to Cindy later.

So Jimbo, using a few euphemisms, makes it clear that Pressy was an enthusiastic participant in the Marshall Plan.

By this time, no one is laughing.

It is a small mercy that Pressy's wife of fifty-some years, Evelyn, passed a few years ago. However, his only son is sitting on the front row. He looks to be in his sixties. He walks up to the podium and tries to take the mic away from Jimbo.

Since the mic's still on, we get treated to most of the play-by-play.

"Why don't you sit down. I think you've said enough," Pressy Junior says.

"I'm just telling it like it is," Jimbo says. He's hanging on to the mic.

"Sit the fuck down," the son says.

"Like hell," says Jimbo.

And then Jimbo gets his feet caught somehow and starts to fall. He grabs Pressy Junior and they both tumble. A couple of guys from the club, here to make sure we don't steal the furniture, move in to separate them.

By the time it's over, Jimbo is complaining about his hip and Pressy Junior has blood trickling from his mouth.

"Just like your old man," we hear Jimbo shout. "Couldn't take a joke."

"Damn," I hear Bootie Carmichael somewhere in front of me, "and they ain't even opened up the bar yet."

"The Marshall Plan," Cindy says.

"I'll tell you later."

* * *

ONCE PEACE has been restored, the combo plays "Georgia on My Mind" because that's where Pressy came from, and we all rush for the bar and the food.

Other than the Jimbo-Pressy Junior battle, the main topic of conversation at the "celebration" is Stick Davis, or rather my involvement with the late Mr. Davis. The story made A1 this morning.

Wheelie and Sarah knew I was working with Stick on his memoirs, with the understanding that I wouldn't be doing anything on company time. We agreed that it would be just as well if Benson Stine was kept in the dark. B.S. believes that his underpaid toilers should spend all their waking hours pursuing good journalism until they are shit-canned in the latest bottom-line bloodletting.

"He probably is going to have a question or two about this," Wheelie understates.

I give the assembled present and former staffers the quick version of the rise and fall of Stick Davis.

* * *

RANDOLPH GILES "Stick" Davis was, or could be, a lot of fun when we were younger. He had a disregard for rules and conventions that made him seem, to some, a romantic figure, the rebel who scoffed at such irritations as class assignments and alarm clocks.

He was a middle-class kid from the North Side. He grew up a block away from Tom Wolfe's boyhood home, although a good bit later. We were both mass com majors at VCU, and, truth be known, I was no slave to others' expectations, either, so we had that in common. And the drinking, of course.

What many of his acquaintances figured out earlier than I did was this: If you don't really give a shit about anybody else's needs, it does not make you a good person, or even a really cool person. As Stick grew older (he never graduated, despite seven years of pretending to be a student), the late, drunken appearances and no-shows eroded affections.

Once, when I was still married to my first wife, Jeanette, I had a rare weekend off, and it was arranged that we, Stick, and his (soon-to-be-ex) wife would go up to the mountains for a couple of days. I had rented a cabin with two bedrooms.

We were supposed to leave at nine Saturday morning. I called Stick at ten, and eleven, and noon. At some point, midafternoon, Jeanette and I took off alone. It was before cell phones, so we had no further contact with Stick until we got back from our abbreviated getaway late Sunday afternoon.

When I called sometime after five, Stick answered the phone.

"Oh, man," he said when I inquired about his absence. "Was that this weekend?"

He didn't even offer to pay his half of the bill for the room.

No saint myself, I stayed with him longer than just about anyone else.

The last straw was back when my third wife, Kate, and I invited him over for drinks and dinner, probably a dozen years ago. He arrived at the Prestwould an hour and a half late and stewed to the gills. Kate's chicken cordon bleu had to be reheated in the microwave, and shortly after we finally sat down to eat, he got up to go to the john, stumbled, and knocked over a nearly full bottle of chardonnay, which went all over the tablecloth and then the floor.

"Sorry," he said.

When I saw him to the door, I was pretty sure I wasn't ever going to see Stick Davis again in a social setting, or at least one at which I played host. Kate reinforced this belief even before the elevator arrived to take him away.

He didn't reenter my life for a long time. Some of us who knew him wondered what happened to him in recent years, but nobody gave enough of a shit to really check it out.

* * *

One night last October, I got a call.

"Hey, man," the voice said. "Long time, no hear."

I was just about to hang up when he told me who it was.

He gave me the short version: He'd been away for a while, like ten years, "Down in the islands, man. Good money down there, I tell you."

He said he was back now, and that he wanted to talk over an idea with me.

"Could be some big bucks in it. More than that damn paper's paying you, I bet."

I could hear his laugh break into a smoker's hack.

I had never benefitted from any of Stick's schemes over the years. He was the one who tried to hook me into selling Amway. He was the one, when we were still in college, who thought I might be interested in going partners with him retailing recreational drugs.

I therefore was a little skeptical. I told Stick I had enough money, a lie, but I was trying to make it clear that whatever he was selling, I wasn't buying.

"Ah, man," he said. "I'm talking about serious money. I'm talking about a book."

I should have hung up. Instead I let him talk.

The book he wanted me to write, or ghost-write, was his autobiography, his "memoirs." I resisted the urge to ask him what he'd ever done that would justify a memoir. I know everybody who can read and write and has hash to settle is writing them now, but Stick Davis's life, or the part about which I knew, was hardly the stuff of best sellers. Recent top-ten lists notwithstanding, being an asshole should not be the only requirement.

He got my attention, though, when he said he'd pay me fifty thousand dollars, five thousand up front. He further piqued my interest with what he said next.

"Timing is kind of essential," he said. "I think I might be on somebody's shit list, if you know what I mean."

I didn't know exactly what he meant, but 5K is 5K, and I figured it couldn't hurt to have a cup of coffee with the guy. So we agreed to meet the next day at the Lamplighter over on Morris Street, an easy walk from the Prestwould.

When I told Cindy about it, she was less than thrilled. She'd heard the stories.

"He doesn't come here," she said. I agreed. Kate, now our landlady, would probably pull the plug on our rental agreement if she knew Stick Davis had set foot inside our unit.

I was at the Lamplighter at ten. Amazingly so was Stick. Had my old drinking buddy finally found a conscience and an alarm clock?

I hadn't seen Stick in more than a decade. In that time, he had, unlike most of us, lost a few pounds. His hair, graying at forty, had magically turned kind of a dirty blond, worn long and shaggy. He had a nasty-looking goatee and a mustache; he seemed to have tanned himself half to death and now was kind of a burnt-orange color. He was wearing sunglasses inside. College students having their morning lattes sneaked stares at him. A dog growled when he walked by.

So, I asked, where the fuck have you been?

He told me. At least he told me some of it.

He'd been back in Richmond for six months "just kind of chilling out, you know."

Sometime after we parted company all those years ago following the unfortunate wine incident, he had moved to the Charlottesville area and managed to get involved with a man named Whitney Charles.

"He was looking for a personal chef, man," Stick said as he poured about a pound of sugar into his coffee. "And I had done some work as a cook at a couple of places. And one night, we were at the same bar and got to talking. Next thing you know, I had a damn job, just cooking for one guy and his guests."

Stick said he did a crash course in gourmet cooking.

"I was actually pretty good at it," he said, kind of wistful, the unspoken part being that Stick was never much good at anything else, including journalism. He said he chose mass communications as his major because 'that's where the chicks are.'

"There was a lot more to it than just cooking," he said.

Whitney Charles, who owned one of those big-ass places you see down in the valley when you're driving through western Albemarle on I-64, decided to relocate.

Stick said "Virgin Gorda" like everybody would know where the hell it was. I had to look it up later on Google Maps. It seemed like the kind of place you went where you weren't expecting or wanting a lot of company.

"Fat virgin," Stick said, laughing. "But nobody much was fat, and there weren't a hell of a lot of virgins around, if you know what I mean."

At any rate, he told me enough about what went on outside the kitchen to make me think Stick Davis maybe had led an interesting enough life to merit a half-assed memoir.

But he wouldn't tell me everything.

"You'll know the whole story when we get there," he said.

Without the other 45K awaiting me when we finished, I'd have told him to take a hike, I guess. I had to admit, though, that he had piqued my interest. Like, for instance, where the hell did Stick Davis, who used to borrow money from anyone stupid enough to loan him any, come up with enough dough to give a newspaper hack that kind of money to write his life story?

I did suggest to Stick that he could do this himself.

He shrugged.

"Aw, hell, Willie. Just because I majored in that shit didn't mean I could write. And you could. Still can. I read the paper."

He handed me a check for five thousand dollars. When I deposited it, it didn't bounce.

And so we began.

I would go over to Stick's rental in Westwood and interview him two or three times a week, then go home and write what I could. I told him that it would work better if I knew where this story was going, but he said wait and see.

❊ ❊ ❊

By the time I've brought my colleagues up to date on the late Stick Davis, a small crowd has gathered around the bar the club set up for us. The staff is starting to put the booze away, so everybody gets one more to go.

"But how does it end?" Ray Long on the copy desk asks.

I take a sip of bourbon and shrug.

"Hell if I know. We never got that far."

"So you didn't bump him off?" Bootie Carmichael asks, grinning.

"I haven't killed anyone in years."

* * *

I DROP Cindy off at the Prestwould before heading in to work. She's a little concerned about my status as a possible suspect in a homicide, but she's kind of preoccupied. Her loving son, Chip, has been sniffing around again, trying to wheedle a loan from his mom.

"He says this time he and his 'associates' have found just the right place for a restaurant," she told me last night. "This one, he says, can't miss."

The last one sure as hell did, I remind her.

The way she says "he says" tells me that she's not buying any of the Chipster's bullshit. Still, it weighs on a mother when she can't give her retirement savings to her feckless son so that he can piss it away.

I pat her knee and tell her I know she'll do the right thing.

"Willie," she says as she opens the passenger-side door on my venerable Honda, "you don't know anything about what might have gotten that guy killed, do you?"

I assure her that I do not.

"Could have been a burglary gone bad," I tell her.

Back at the paper, ready to cover whatever mayhem a pleasant Tuesday evening might bring to the night police beat, I think about it.

Leighton Byrd comes by to thank me for letting her write the story of Stick Davis's demise. I remind her that, from this point on, this baby is mine.

She seems miffed, but the fetching Leighton will have to pad her résumé elsewhere, assuming I can keep my ass out of jail. This story has more legs than a millipede.

A botched burglary is a reasonable explanation, but they don't happen that much in the part of Richmond where Stick was renting. And even in the rare break-in gone bad, the victim usually isn't turned into Swiss cheese and used as an ashtray.

Somebody didn't like Stick Davis very much, is my belief at this point. He had hinted that he might have some enemies.

Or maybe he just showed up late one time too many.

CHAPTER THREE

Wednesday, September 4

Maybe leaving Stick Davis's body where I found it, carefully wiping the doorknob and anything else I touched, and letting somebody else discover it when it started to smell might not have been the worst idea. No good deed, etc.

I got a call from one of L.D. Jones's detectives first thing this morning. Could I come down to headquarters to clear up a couple of matters regarding Randolph Giles Davis?

Well, of course I could. Nothing would please me more, except maybe a colonoscopy without anesthesia.

L.D.'s empire is only a few blocks away. I detour to pay a visit to the esteemed law practice of Green and Ellis. Marcus Green, the town's most self-promoting ambulance chaser, is now partner, in business and in bed, with Kate Ellis, my third and second-to-last wife. She opted not to change her name, maybe to honor the memory of the husband she married and then lost between me and Marcus due to the unfortunate merger of an airplane with a local eatery.

Marcus and I help each other out occasionally, and there are no hard feelings about the bed thing. Hell, I even went to their wedding.

"I wondered how long it'd take you to show up," Marcus says when I walk into their little two-lawyers-and-an-aide operation on Franklin. He is immaculate in his three-piece suit. His mahogany head looks like he polished it this morning. He seems to be smirking. "I knew you were a bad man, Willie, but murder?"

He lets go with that rumbling, baritone laugh of his. Obviously Marcus thinks this is a hell of a lot funnier than I do.

I tell him what he already knows, that I might need a lawyer.

"Don't know if you can afford me," he says.

He pauses for effect.

"Just kiddin'. We'll work something out."

Marcus often takes cases on the cheap, or even pro bono, if they promise to enhance his image as the man to see if you've done something really bad and can pay big bucks to make it go away. Now that Kate's his partner, they've had to tweak the TV ad you see every five damn minutes during the evening news around here. The new one: "Want to get ruthless? Call Green and Ellis." It is my opinion that Kate does not scowl nearly as well as Marcus in the video, although in our years of marital bliss, she did have plenty of opportunities to work on her frown lines.

Marcus asks me if I want him to come with me to this morning's session with the cops. I tell him I'll handle this one on my own, that I want to know how damn serious the police are about me being a suspect.

Kate comes out of her office and says hello, among other things.

"You didn't tell me that you were on speaking terms with that jerk again," she says, giving me a pretty good scowl.

I assure her that Stick Davis has not been inside the unit she's renting to us and that I haven't forgotten the infamous chardonnay incident.

"If I'd had a gun," she mutters, as she turns around, "I'd have shot him myself."

"Take care, Willie," Marcus says when he shows me out. "Don't say anything you'll wish you hadn't later."

I'm not too worried about that. There aren't a lot of perks to being night police reporter, but knowing how the cops operate is one of them.

* * *

I drive down to the paper and park in the lot I'm paying for already, then take the one-Camel walk back to police headquarters.

The chief wants to sit in on this one. L.D. and a couple of his detectives invite me into a too-small room where, I am assured, smoking is not permitted, although a little nicotine might improve the smell of the place.

"We just want to get the facts straight," the bigger one, a white guy with a mustache and a beer gut, says. "Just tell us what happened."

The other one just nods his head. I don't think they're dumb enough to try good-cop, bad-cop on me, but who knows?

And so I start to explain it all again. I take out my notebook, where I wrote it all down two days ago, just to be sure there are no inconsistencies.

"You're not sure what happened?" the other dick, a black guy who is about five foot six and weighs maybe 120 pounds, asks. He seems to adopt something between a smirk and a sneer.

I just stare.

"Go on," the chief says. I just look at him and shake my head, then continue.

When I'm done, they ask me a few questions designed to trip me up, trying to cast doubt about the time frame, inquiring again as to whether I'd seen Stick since we last met in person on Thursday.

"And you'd never been in the deceased's home until you went in and allegedly found the body on September 2."

I slam my right fist down on the table, startling the two detectives and causing L.D. to spill some coffee on his shirt.

"I just told you three goddamn minutes ago that we met at his apartment several times over the last few months, to go over what I'd written so far," I explain with all the calmness and civility these idiots deserve. "Aren't you listening?"

The big one seems to be in favor of giving me a good Tasing, but the chief motions for him to back off.

I tell them about Stick mentioning, back when this whole project started, that he might have an enemy or two out there. Nobody seems to take much interest in that.

They ask a few more inane questions. Then they slap their little notebooks shut.

"We'll be speaking with you later," the short one says. "Don't leave town."

I tell him he'll be leaving town before I do, and that the next time we meet, I'll have Marcus Green with me.

"Only a man with something to hide gets a lawyer," the big one says.

"Only a fool doesn't," I reply.

After the detectives leave, L.D. asks me to hang back.

"Do you really think I killed Stick Davis?" I ask my old frenemy.

He sighs.

"Willie, I don't believe or disbelieve. I just go with the facts. And we don't know of anybody who'd had contact with Mr. Davis recently except you."

I express the hope that he and his minions are trying to find alternative suspects. He assures me that they are.

I note that I don't even own a gun. The only one I've had in my whole life I turned in during one of those police department buy-backs years ago.

"People borrow guns," the chief says.

"Do you know how crazy this is?"

L.D. doesn't answer at first.

"Willie," he says when he clears his throat. "Do you remember that guy that was murdering those young black boys around here a few years back?"

Hell, I should, since I helped show the cops that the late James Alderman was a stone psychopath.

"Well," he goes on, "that man was a so-called pillar of the community, and we find out he was slaughtering little kids."

"Your point?"

He looks at me and shakes his head.

"You never know," he says. "You just never know."

We leave it at that. I advise him to get smarter detectives, and then I leave.

I'm sure something, DNA or a witness or something, will clear all this up. Still, it pisses me off.

* * *

Back at the word factory, there is reason to hope that our publisher will be distracted from reading me the riot act over (a) doing freelance work on the side without telling him and (b) managing to make myself the prime suspect in a murder case.

"We don't have enough homicides around here, you've got to start doing them yourself?" Sally Velez asks, not looking up. I emphasize to her how much I am not amused.

The shiny object that I pray will distract Benson Stine from chewing on my ass is a hurricane.

We get all quivery around here when there's a storm somewhere between the Cape Verde islands and downtown Richmond. And this one looks like it might justify the fact that we now have a full-time weather reporter. Dorian hit somewhere in the Bahamas with 185-mile-per-hour winds three days ago, and now it's treading water out there in the Atlantic like a mean drunk trying to decide who to hit next.

Yesterday it started moving in our general direction, causing a serious run on water, toilet paper, beer, Cheetos, and other necessities.

Usually these things skirt the coast and wind up in Nova Scotia or some damn where else up north. On the off chance that this one will head straight for the holy city, though, we are overplaying the shit out of it. Maps, predictions, interviews with idiots in line at the grocery store, updates on Dominion Power's plans for after the apocalypse. We've got it all. Hey, it sells papers. Our readers would much rather read about possible death and destruction than peruse some happy-news piece about people trying to make the world a better place.

And so I find the newsroom a relative whirlwind of activity. I say "relative" because it's hard to stir up a big media storm when you only have about a third of the people we had back when newspapers were relevant and turned a profit.

Still we try. The weather guy, who's about half my age and is, I understand, making about as much as I am, is scurrying around like he runs the place. Hell, from the way B.S. is sitting there, letting him order people about, maybe he does.

The kid is dressed for heavy weather, even though the sun's shining here. He's headed down to the Outer Banks so he can feel Dorian's vibe firsthand.

"Sure would hate to have something happen to the weather guy," I hear Enos Jackson mutter. That's actually what everyone calls him: Weather Guy. His real name is Guy Flowers, but hardly anybody calls him that. It's either Weather Guy, or W.G.

Unfortunately, Stine spots me before I can duck into the snack room. He is walking in my direction, and it seems like bad form to turn and run. What the hell. Might as well face the music.

He motions me into the managing editor's office. Wheelie, our ME, is, as usual, in a meeting elsewhere.

"So," our publisher says, "I understand that we're not paying you enough."

"Have I asked for a raise?" I inquire.

"You have not," he says. "And it would have been a waste of time if you had. No raises until we turn the bottom line around."

I don't mention that making a print newspaper turn a good profit these days would be too much even for a competent publisher who didn't work for the Grimm Group, hands-down the stingiest media chain in North America.

"So you just decided to give yourself a raise," he says.

I point out that not one damn minute of the time I spent working on Stick Davis's memoirs was stolen from the company.

"What if there had been a triple homicide when you were working on this character's so-called memoirs?"

I have the answer for that one, except it was a double homi. It happened three weeks ago, and I stopped writing the Stick Davis story long enough, on one of my alleged days off, to rush over to the East End and cover it.

"Well," B.S. says, "that might be the case, but . . ."

"It is the case. If I say it was the case, dammit, it is the case."

"Just a figure of speech," Stine says, backing up a little. "But now you've got us dragged into a murder story. We aren't here to make the news, Willie, we're supposed to be here to cover it."

How, I inquire, am I supposed to be responsible for the city cops thinking I killed somebody?

"Don't be at the scene of the crime?" he suggests. "Don't be the only one known to have seen Mr. Davis in the days before his death? I can think of lots of ways, Willie."

I've taken my full quota of crap about something I didn't do.

"If you really think I'm a liability to this paper, or I've been stealing time from it," I tell B.S., "then do what you have to do. Meanwhile I'm going to do my job, assuming I still have one."

I turn to walk out of the office, wondering if the parting words from our publisher will be "You're fired."

Instead, Stine says, "Just get this mess cleared up. It's making the paper look bad."

I resist the urge to do a U-ey and make Benson Stine's nose look bad. Hell, I need the job.

There isn't much to do except try to find out what really happened to Stick Davis. During all the sessions we had after I agreed to ghostwrite his memoirs, he never said anything solid about enemies he might have accumulated over the years, just that one hint about someone or ones he'd pissed off.

We had gotten to the part where he found himself a benefactor, Whitney Charles, and followed him down to the Caribbean, specifically to Virgin Gorda. Stick had told me a lot about his sexual adventures down there, many of them not age-appropriate, and a little about some of the things he was doing for Charles acting as what Stick called his majordomo. He was still a little coy about what exactly he did do, but it was pretty obvious that, unless the laws in the British Virgin Islands were drastically different than they are in Virginia, felonies were committed.

How, I asked Stick, is all this going to turn into something that will make it worthwhile for you to pay me fifty thousand dollars to write it?

"Just wait," he said. "The good stuff is coming."

Halfway through, I was still waiting for the good stuff when somebody made Stick Davis dead.

* * *

It's too early in the day for much mayhem to erupt, so I slip out from hurricane central.

I drive over to Westwood. There's yellow crime tape around the door of the place Skip was renting, and I see that there's a cop car outside. I figured that would be the case, but it doesn't hurt to try.

Despite the impending killer hurricane, it's a pretty nice day. I delay trying to get into the scene of the crime long enough to drive around the neighborhood.

It's hard to imagine what it must have looked like, back when it was a tucked-away haven for former slaves, far enough away from Richmond to have its own identity. It's a little sliced-up these days, and a lot of the houses that still stand have been added on to.

From what I hear, a lot of the folks who come to services at the Baptist church live elsewhere now, scattered to the winds but still faithful to their parents' and grandparents' church.

I watch some kids playing basketball on the church's outdoor courts and contemplate Stick Davis.

There must be something somewhere in his last dwelling that could tell me how the hell all this happened.

I drive back to Stick's place and park.

The cops, two of them, are still there, sitting in their squad car. When I walk up and lean into the driver's-side window, I see the face of my old pal Chauncey Gillespie.

"Any chance I could get in there and take a look?" I ask, knowing what the answer will be.

Gillespie just laughs.

"So you can destroy evidence?"

I tell him that there are some notebooks in there that I need to get my hands on.

Stick alluded more than once to his notebooks, as if all would be revealed in those sacred texts.

Gillespie and his partner not only won't let me inside, they won't even let me get close enough to peek in the windows.

"No donuts for you," I admonish my old pal, who tells me to get the fuck out of there.

I'll get into Stick's place somehow, but not today.

There's nothing else to do but go back to the office and await the demonic Dorian.

CHAPTER FOUR

Thursday, September 5

Last night was quiet, by Richmond mayhem standards.

Nothing really felonious was brought to my attention. A couple of poor saps went off an exit ramp in a pickup just beyond where I-95 crosses the river and became very dead, but nobody told us about it until this morning. A guy out in Chesterfield caught a couple of kids rifling through his car for pocket change and thought that gave him the right to shoot them. Luckily he missed, succeeding in blowing out his own windshield and getting his own ass arrested, but that's not my bailiwick.

So I had time to do a little checking up on the late Mr. Davis.

I was able to find one family member. Through my reliable cops source, Peachy Love, reporter turned police flack, I got the name of what passes for next of kin—one George Davis.

"I think he goes by 'Snake,'" Peachy said, and she gave me his address.

Apparently the cops contacted the guy on Tuesday and got him to go down to the morgue and identify his brother.

"The officer I talked to said he didn't seem all that broken up."

The brother told the cops that their parents were dead.

"He seemed concerned that he might have to pay for burial expenses," Peachy said.

Stick and Snake, I'm thinking. With nicknames like that, they should've grown up down the street from me in Oregon Hill.

Three times, I tried the number Peachy gave me. Finally, sometime after nine, I got an answer.

George "Snake" Davis, I knew from the records I'd looked up after talking to Peachy, was born in 1952, making him eight years older than Stick. He wasn't guilty of anything worse, the record showed, than a couple of DUIs. I can hardly fault him for that. Glass houses and all.

I explained who I was and tried to build some rapport with Mr. Davis, who seemed to be a few sheets into the wind.

"Do you know anything about the funeral?" I asked.

He wasn't terribly forthcoming. He figured I had an angle and was somehow going to cost him money.

Finally, though, I got it through his thick skull that I was only trying to find out what happened to his damn brother.

"You the one that found him?" Snake asked, although I imparted that information five minutes earlier.

"Well," he said after I had confirmed that I was indeed the one, "he was shot up pretty good, wasn't he?"

Yes, I agreed, he was.

I asked again about the funeral.

"Oh, that's all taken care of."

I have some knowledge of what funerals cost. I pressed for more information.

"The fella he worked for, down there in the islands. He sent a certified check."

"Whit Charles?"

"Yeah. That's the one. Don't even know how he knew Stick died. But I got word from the morgue that he had somehow found out. They wanted me to make the arrangements."

I asked about those arrangements. After the autopsy, Stick Davis had been cremated, his brother told me, but there will be a small gathering at O'Toole's, a fine drinking and eating establishment not far from where Snake lives, on Saturday.

"And he paid to have something put in the paper. I give 'em all the information I knew. And I let that girl know, the one he's been seeing."

OK, I knew Stick had a girlfriend out there somewhere, but I never met her. I had to get her name from Snake, who also had her phone number. Terri McAllister. I wrote down the number.

"Do you know why anybody would want to kill your brother?" I inquired.

George Davis laughed, kind of a sad laugh, I thought.

"Oh, Stick, he was always gettin' on somebody's bad side. I suppose he finally picked the wrong one to piss off."

He hadn't known much if any more about what his brother had been up to for the past decade or so than I had.

"I'd get a Christmas card from him, usually in January. He hinted about having something big going on down there, but I never could get him to tell me what exactly. I seen him maybe three times since he come back here."

Snake had no contact information for Whitney Charles, either, just his name on a certified check.

I asked if it would be OK if I came to the affair at O'Toole's, and Snake said that'd be fine.

"The more the merrier. Hell, I don't even know if Stick had ever been to O'Toole's, but that's where I hang out, and that girl, Terri, she knows where it is."

I wondered who else would be there for a guy who seemed to have left almost no footprints in Richmond at all.

* * *

THIS MORNING, the obit's in the paper. He's listed as Randolph Giles "Stick" Davis, and his whole life is summed up in fifteen lines. Who his parents were, who his brother is, his "special friend" Terri McAllister, that he attended VCU, and was working in "international finance." Snake must have pulled that one straight out of his ass. They give the time and place for a "celebration" on Saturday. When I die, I don't want people to celebrate. I want wailing and gnashing of teeth.

I think that I could have added a little information, but at least, with the obit in the paper, maybe an old friend or two will show up, if Stick still had any.

Cindy's gone already when I get up. I'm perusing Stick's obit at the breakfast table, with Butterball perched at my feet, hoping for a few crumbs, when the phone rings.

The voice, like distant thunder, is unmistakable. Franklin "Big Boy" Sunday.

"Wanted you to know," he rumbles. "They got Jerome in jail for killing that fella."

"What fella?"

"The one you was supposed to of killed."

Enlighten me, I implore.

Jerome is Jerome Sheets, who is or was one of Big Boy's henchmen/drivers. He might have driven me the few times I've been uneasily in the company of his boss. All of Big Boy's drivers looked as if they would have liked to have fucked me up just for being partly white.

Sometime after ten last night, the cops caught young Jerome, who is seventeen years old, allegedly breaking and entering at a place over east of Libbie, between Patterson and Broad. He made a run for it, but they caught him. He'd thrown the bag with whatever he'd stolen into a ditch, but they found that soon enough.

It was what else they found that has the kid in deep shit.

"He was wearing the man's watch," Big Boy says. "Had that Davis guy's initials on it and everything. Some cop was smart enough to see the initials and had a hunch."

Yes, I remember that watch. Stick was proud as hell of it, said it was worth five thousand dollars, which I doubted. Still, quite the watch.

Late in the evening, acting on that hunch, the city's legal brain trust was able to get a judge to issue a search warrant for Jerome's mom's place. Sometime in the middle of the night, Big Boy says, they did the search. They found, among other things, Stick Davis's wallet and his VCU class ring. I'm amazed that the cops didn't notice his lack of jewelry or billfold on Monday. I'm amazed that I didn't, considering how much Stick thought of that watch.

There were some unidentified fingerprints at the scene. Some will be mine, but it seems highly likely that some of them will be found to belong to Jerome Sheets.

"The thing is," Big Boy says, after I hear him yell to somebody to bring him some more coffee, "I don't believe the boy did it."

As the previous prime suspect, this is not what I want to hear.

"Aw, hell, Willie," my caller says, laughing, "I don't think you killed the fella either. No offense, but you ain't got the balls to go shoot somebody up like that."

I don't know whether to be offended or not.

"But Jerome, he ain't no killer. Hell, I've known that boy since he was a baby. He acts tough. Got to act tough where he comes from. But he ain't no killer. Hell, I don't even let him pack. Don't need anybody shootin' people up while they're in my employ. Bad for business."

I have my doubts about Big Boy Sunday's assertion but keep it to myself.

So Jerome Sheets is down at the lockup now, and I'm sure that word will get out very soon about a press conference this morning. When white folks get murdered in their own residences, L.D. Jones wants it known ASAP that the perp has been caught.

I thank Big Boy for giving me a head start on this one.

"Well," he says, drawing it out to three syllables, "there is a little tit for tat here, if you know what I mean."

Big Boy enlightens me.

He would consider it a very big favor if I'd look into this miscarriage of justice and try to ensure that Jerome doesn't go to the death house for something he didn't do.

"He's been known to do a little burglary, now and then, but he ain't no killer."

I ask my caller how exactly I'm supposed to effect what he sees as justice.

"You got a reputation, Willie," he explains. "I know you won't stop just because the po-po say they got the right one this time. I'm counting on you, Willie."

It is not wise to disappoint Big Boy Sunday. His boy Jerome might not be a killer, but Big Boy's got a few associates who sure as hell are.

I ask him again why he's so sure Jerome didn't do the deed. He could, I suggest, have surprised Stick and been forced to shoot him. I mean, we have kids younger than him doing the deed all the time around these parts.

"I talked to his momma," Big Boy says.

Jerome's mother swears that her son has never owned a gun and hadn't ever even fired one.

"And I believe her," he adds. "I believe her because me and her been what you would call intimate for years, and

I know she told me the truth. She knows it wouldn't be smart to do otherwise. Plus, I know that boy."

What can I do? I promise Big Boy Sunday that I will do the best I can.

"I know you, Willie," the big man says. "I know you will."

* * *

I DON'T wait to get a call from the office about a press conference. It's too much fun to call L.D. Jones in person.

"Tell him," I inform his aide, "that I want to talk to him about Jerome Sheets."

The chief is on the line in no time at all.

"You don't know shit," he says by way of greeting. "This doesn't get you off the hook. I hope you know that."

I then tell him pretty much what I know he's going to tell the assembled and shrinking news media in a couple of hours: Kid from the East End was arrested wearing Stick Davis's watch. They found his wallet and class ring in his mother's house after getting a late-night search warrant.

"All I need to know," I tell L.D., "is whether or not the fingerprints match."

"You'll get it when everybody else does," the chief says. "And if I ever find out who's feeding you this shit, he's going to be a school safety guard for the rest of his natural police life."

I make a deal with him. If he'll let me take a quick look around the deceased's study, I won't post anything on our website until after the press conference. It's a dicey deal, I know, but who the hell is going to care whether our readers learn this scintillating detail now or two hours later? These days, we are much more concerned with being first than being right, but I can always tell Sarah and Wheelie, if they find out I knew ahead of time, that I was just trying to make sure.

And I really need to get into that study.

L.D. is quiet for several seconds.

"Fifteen minutes," he says when he finally answers. "And my men will be watching you like a goddamn hawk. You mess with evidence and I will mess you up."

I agree with the chief's rules.

So, I ask, am I free to leave the country now?

"You stay right where the hell you are," he growls.

I wish the chief a nice day and say that I'll see him soon, at the press conference.

* * *

THE PRESSER is at ten thirty. The chief assures the media that a "person of interest" is now behind bars, pending further investigation.

"Is Willie Black still a suspect?" one of the TV riffraff asks, a grin on his well-tanned face.

"Nothing has changed on that front," L.D. replies, not looking in my direction.

I file for the website from my car, then head straight to the place in Westwood.

A couple of cops I don't know are guarding it, and they look at me like I've got an extra head when I tell them the chief said I could look around. They won't let me in until I finally get L.D. on the phone and he tells them it's OK. They are less than thrilled about it.

"Your fifteen minutes just started," one of them says to me as I slip under the yellow crime tape and we walk inside. I'm sure he'll be timing me to the second.

I poke around for what I should have looked for last Monday but kind of got caught up in the moment.

They aren't there.

Stick had kept notebooks, lots of them. He would refer to them sometimes when we were collaborating, but he wouldn't let me look at them. The way it worked, he'd refer to the notebooks and tell me what he wanted me to write. I'd turn his ramblings into something publishable and then run the results past Stick. Then we'd get together at his place and he'd tell me what he did or didn't like about what I'd done. It was a fairly amicable if tedious working relationship, but whenever I wanted to know what came next, or what was in all those notebooks, he turned into the goddamn sphinx.

I walk around the tape outlining the position of Stick's fallen body, the carpet pretty much permanently ruined by his blood. I look around the desk and check all the drawers as the two cops bird-dogging me keep warning me not to take anything. There's no sign of the notebooks.

Peachy Love has given me a good description of what the police found in that sack Jerome Sheets threw out, and what was hidden at his mom's place, and there was nothing about any notebooks. And why the hell would a junior felon bother with stealing paper anyhow?

I have more than a hundred pages of the Stick Davis story on my computer at home, saved on Gmail as well, but we were just getting to the good stuff, I thought, when Stick's clock ran out.

Stick was renting the place from some folks who bought it as an investment. It is a nice place: good-sized living room, the study, a small kitchen-dining room, two bedrooms, one bath, and a nice deck out back. I see nothing in any of those rooms that I'm looking for.

"Time's up," the lead cop says much too soon.

I tell him he's been a big help. He doesn't seem to understand sarcasm.

* * *

My head is spinning. I know I didn't kill Stick Davis, and I'm pretty sure that somebody other than Jerome Sheets has been rummaging around in Davis's office between the last time I saw him alive and my finding the body. And why is Whit Charles springing for the funeral expenses of his former major (or at least minor) domo?

While I ponder all this, there's plenty of time to give my old mom a visit before heading into the office.

Peggy is, well, Peggy. She is, as she so elegantly puts it, "seventy-fucking-seven years old." She is wearing a T-shirt and jeans. The T-shirt is Grateful Dead-themed, circa 1975, which is probably when she bought it. And she is, as usual, mildly stoned.

If they ever do a comprehensive study of the effect of long-term marijuana use on a person's lungs, brain, and other parts, my mother should be Exhibit A.

She managed to hold a variety of jobs as I was growing up under her single parentage, and she always seemed to be there for me. I was probably in my mid-teens before I realized that her affinity for Oreos and her mellow outlook toward even the cruelest of life's tricks was not organic, unless you count the fact that cannabis is a plant.

It didn't really bother me. There were lots worse mothers than Peggy on the Hill back then, trust me. And despite it all, she's in better shape than I am. She says I'm smoking the wrong thing.

Peggy and Awesome Dude, her permanent and platonic (please God, let it be platonic) houseguest, are watching some cooking show on one of the umpteen channels devoted to food.

"That's making me hungry," Peggy says as she watches some woman whip up a four-course dinner for eight without seeming to break a sweat.

Then she remembers that her darling boy has been making the news lately, and not in a good way.

"You didn't kill that fella, did you?" she asks.

"Nah," Awesome interjects. "Willie wouldn't kill nobody."

I assure them both that this is true and let them know that Richmond's finest have found a more likely suspect.

"Well, I didn't think you did," Peggy says and offers me a Miller, the family beverage.

She says she called me right after the news broke that I was a suspect "but then I kind of forgot about it." I tell her no harm, no foul.

She gets out some cold cuts and the three of us have lunch. I try to keep an eye on my mom to make sure she isn't drifting into an area where she'll need more help than the feckless Dude can give her, but I can't detect anything. Since Peggy is a little bit buzzed all the time, it might be hard to tell when and if real and true dementia sets in.

She assures me that all is well with Andi, Walter, and young William, my five-year old grandson and light of our lives. Andi did call me after the news broke about Stick Davis, and I have assured her that her dad's not going to the slammer.

I give my mom a little rundown on Stick, going back to the days when he managed to eventually alienate most of his friends.

"He sounds like an asshole," is Peggy's assessment. "What the hell were you doing working with a guy like that?"

"Money."

"Yeah, money can screw things up," she says. "Luckily I never let it ruin me."

She laughs loud enough to disturb the neighbors.

* * *

I come to work a little early. There's the story on Jerome Sheets to write, plus I'd like to do something more on

Stick Davis, like why a guy from the British Virgin Islands is springing for his funeral expenses.

Our publisher comes by and pats me on the back.

"I knew you didn't do it," he says, in a way that indicates that he wasn't sure at all until Jerome Sheets's arrest. I remind him that I'm not in the clear yet. He frowns and walks away.

The newsroom rumor mill is working overtime. The latest gossip has it that deadlines are going to be moved up.

This has been a sore point for years, especially among the boys and girls in Toyland, the sports department. Every time we are gifted with a new technological breakthrough, the deadlines seem to get tighter.

Bootie Carmichael can remember when our city-edition readers were privy to the previous night's West Coast baseball box scores. Now they're lucky if they get all the East Coast games.

And, as we have learned, things can get worse—apparently are getting worse. Starting soon, rumor has it, the lockup for our last (and now only) edition will be ten P.M. That means a nine thirty deadline for copy. If a college hoops game starts shortly after seven and there are the requisite number of TV timeouts, we figure the hapless sportswriter will have about five minutes to write the game story.

And, of course, we will have to politely request that our local felons start shooting each other a little earlier in the evening.

We will, as usual, tell the readers that they can read all about it on our handy online website, for free until they hit the firewall, at which point most of them just go to another site.

A cynic might think we didn't want to be pestered with putting out a print newspaper, with all that expensive paper and all those costly freelance carriers.

Will the last print subscriber please turn off the printing presses?

After I finish my piece on Jerome Sheets's arrest, I have to hustle out to the scene of a shooting on Chamberlayne Avenue. Two young men, allegedly minding their own business, were sprayed coming out of a place specializing in hot wings. One of them is not expected to make it. Nobody in the fairly crowded eatery saw anything.

I do manage to squeeze in a couple of hours to do a little online research on Whitney Charles.

Mr. Charles, who seems to prefer "Whit," appeared in our electronic files a few times before he left the commonwealth in 2005. He was and presumably is a lawyer. He was involved in a few development deals around Charlottesville that were mentioned by our business department, and he made the state and local front three times that I could find because he seemed to be a little careless with some of his clients' money. He managed to get himself named guardian for several of them, and the clients' heirs, upon getting the final accounting, wondered where the hell all of Uncle Fred's life savings went.

There were threats of lawsuits and even disbarment, but apparently Whit was able to dodge the bullet.

The last word we had on Whit Charles was a piece in the Home section about him selling his place in Albemarle County for a couple of million in 2005. The story quoted Mr. Charles as saying he was taking some time off to sail the Caribbean.

I figure Whit Charles set off for paradise about three years before he and Stick Davis met and Stick subsequently went south. Obviously Mr. Charles made a few trips back to Virginia between 2005 and 2008, because Stick said they connected in Charlottesville during that time. He didn't do anything in the Old Dominion recently to earn himself a mention in our newspaper though.

I was able, with a little help from Ed Chenowith, who knows how to find shit, to get an address and a phone number for Whit Charles down in Virgin Gorda.

He'll be getting a wakeup call from me tomorrow.

CHAPTER FIVE

Friday, September 6

I call Whit Charles's number on Virgin Gorda shortly after nine A.M., which I figure will be ten o'clock island time.

A man with an island lilt to his English answers. No, Mr. Charles is not home. He is traveling. No, no one is sure when he will be back. When I ask if Mr. Charles is by chance in the United States, specifically in the state of Virginia, the man pauses and then says that he isn't authorized to say, and neither is anyone else at Chez Charles.

Despite the fact that Whit Charles or someone authorized by him sent a certified check up here a few days ago to pay for Stick Davis's funeral, my trusty reporter's instincts tell me the man is somewhere in the commonwealth, maybe even in Richmond. I mean, if you're going to pay for some underling's funeral, wouldn't you be a good bet to take the trouble to show up?

* * *

THE COPS confirm that the fingerprints match. Jerome Sheets definitely was in Stick Davis's house in the recent past. That plus the goods with which he was caught red-handed would seem to seal the deal for ol' Jerome, who claims he was just there for a burglary and didn't have anything to do with any shooting. There were other prints besides Jerome's and mine, but nobody knows who those belong to, and nobody seems to much care.

Peachy Love tells me, on the down-low, that the kid says the place was unlocked when he dropped by to burglarize it on Saturday night, making it likely that he was testing every unlit dwelling on the block, hoping to get lucky. He told the cops he saw the body but was afraid to report it. Not too afraid, it seems, to steal what he could.

I call Marcus Green. I suggest that Jerome Sheets might need his services more than I do.

"Off the hook, huh?" he says.

I express some doubts about Jerome's guilt, evidence to the contrary.

"He might deserve some major time for burglary, but I'm not sure he did the killing."

"Man," Marcus says, "you just want to be the contrarian, don't you? Not satisfied with getting off the Number One suspect hot seat. You just want to show up L.D. Jones and the police department."

"Only if they're wrong."

"Yeah," he says. "But this one sounds like it'd be a fool's errand. Plus, who's going to pay me?"

I mention that Jerome is under the protective wing of Big Boy Sunday.

"Good God. That guy. Just working for him makes the kid a viable suspect for just about any crime you want to think of."

"Yeah," I reply, "but Big Boy will pay well to see him get off the murder rap."

Big Boy has been a client of Marcus's in the past, the result of some unfortunate incidents in which I am sure Big Boy was blameless. Marcus knows there'll be a payday out of this, beyond the free publicity he craves.

He does have one concern though.

"Big Boy doesn't like it much when his people go to jail. What if I'm right and this is Occam's Razor—the obvious answer is the right one?"

"Well," I tell my old buddy, "then I guess he'll just have to kill you."

Despite his qualms, I have the feeling that Marcus finds this case irresistible.

* * *

I CHECK in at the office. The weather seems strangely placid for an area anticipating the storm of the century.

Sally Velez confirms what I gathered from the early morning weather-rama on TV. They still were giving the usual warnings, but the weather map told the story. We have dodged the bullet, as we usually do. Dorian, we hardly knew ye.

"Weather Guy is still somewhere on the Outer Banks," she says. "They've told him to come on back, but he says there's still time for the hurricane to make a hard left turn."

"Wishful thinking."

"Yeah. I'm sure he's a little depressed that oak trees aren't falling through people's roofs up here."

Hell, Weather Guy isn't much if any worse than the rest of us. Who didn't get a journalistic woody when those planes hit the World Trade Towers and the Pentagon and we spent a solid week working twelve-hour days covering something that really mattered? The mass murders at Virginia Tech? It seemed like half the damn newsroom headed for Blacksburg to hound the bereaved.

Weather Guy knows that he's not going to make his bones around here on sunny and warm.

With Dorian headed for points north, there is time in the quiet late morning to do a little checking up on Stick.

The message box is full on McAllister's phone when I call. She works as a waitress "somewhere around here, in the Fan, I think," according to Snake.

Abe Custalow to the rescue. I'm talking about the case with my sub-lessee and lifelong friend, who drops by our shared domicile sometimes between errands. He's in charge of maintenance at the Prestwould, and work breaks are hard to come by. The building is ninety years old and acts its age sometimes.

"Terri McAllister?" he says when I mention the girlfriend's name. "Yeah, I think Stella knows her. Just a minute."

Sometimes Richmond seems like a very small town. If you don't know somebody, you know somebody who does.

Abe's soon conversing with Stella Stellar, his main squeeze. Stella and her band, the melodious Goldfish Crackers, are trying with middling success to crack the big-time. When they're in town, Abe sometimes keeps her sheets warm.

"Yeah. That's what I thought. She's the one, huh? She's where? OK. Thanks."

He hangs up and gives me the name of the eatery on West Main where's she's waitressing.

I pay the place a visit. It's had four different names and owners in my memory. Hope springs eternal.

They're getting ready for the lunch crowd, which might be a little light, since everyone hasn't gotten the word yet that Richmond will not be wiped from the face of the earth by the killer hurricane. (Yes, it is a killer. Some guy down in North Carolina fell off a ladder putting up storm shutters and broke his neck.)

* * *

TERRI MCALLISTER looks to be in the general vicinity of fifty years old, far too long of tooth to be slinging hash in this place on West Main that apparently only serves food in order to keep its liquor license.

She, like the late Stick, has tinted her hair a bit, but her dark roots are showing. Unlike Stick, she could use a membership at the Y, although waiting tables looks to me like it'd be a good way to lose weight. One of her arms is tattooed as far up as I can see.

I catch her before the place starts filling up, and she grudgingly gives me five minutes.

I express my sorrow at her loss.

"Yeah," she says, shrugging. "Stick was OK. I'm gonna miss him."

She doesn't seem excessively distraught over her boyfriend's passing.

I ask how long they'd been "seeing" each other.

"Oh, since May, no April. Yeah."

Then she puts two and two together.

"Willie Black. Shit. You're the son of a bitch they said killed him," she says, using her outdoor voice and drawing attention from the two habituals at the bar. "What the hell are you doing out of jail?"

I explain, as quickly and quietly as I can, that I was the one who found him, that he and I were working on a book and that the police have arrested someone else they suspect committed the crime.

"You mean to say some little shit shot him all that many times and burned him just because he wanted to rob him? Hell, I can't see Stick putting up a fight over anything in that place."

I tell her that, from what I can learn, there didn't seem to be any resistance on his part.

Finally mollified that I didn't kill her boyfriend, she motions for me to follow her outside.

"I'm coming back, goddammit," she explains to a frowny-faced young man who must be the manager.

Outside, she walks me down half a block and into the garbage-scented alley that bisects it. She and I both light up.

"Stick was afraid," she says.

"About what?"

"I dunno, exactly. But he told me one time that it'd be a good thing if I didn't spread his name around town. He said he'd made an enemy or two."

I note that Stick sometimes had a knack for making enemies.

She laughs.

"True dat. I mean, he was always good to me, but you could tell, the way he acted, that there was people he'd just as soon not run into."

When I ask for more details, she either doesn't have any or won't share them.

"I kind of knew he was working on some kind of book," she says, "but he wouldn't tell me shit about it."

She stamps out her cigarette.

"You going to the service tomorrow?" she asks.

"Plan to."

"I don't know who all is going to be there. I swear, Stick didn't seem to have any other friends around Richmond. I was surprised when he said he grew up here. Didn't seem much into reconnecting or any such shit. He had his brother, who seems like kind of an asshole, but I don't know when he ever saw him."

She says he met her at Bandito's, and they kind of hit it off, but afterward he was mostly a homebody.

"We hung out, you know. I'd stay over at his place over on Stokes Lane sometimes, and he'd usually just order takeout."

She lowers her voice a little although there's nobody except a no-tail alley cat in the near vicinity.

"He said something about having some money," she says. "And he did give me some nice shit. Gave me this little necklace for my birthday."

She shows me what appears to be an actual diamond hanging around her neck, the chain bisecting a barbed-wire tattoo.

"He didn't say anything about, like a will or something, did he?"

I give Terri the sad news that, no, I know nothing about a will. It is hard for me to imagine Stick, either the Stick I knew long ago or the one with whom I was passingly familiar recently, going to all that trouble.

"We weren't, you know, serious. Not really," she says. "He was good company, most of the time, but I don't think whatever we were doing was going anywhere."

Tough old girl that she appears to be, she seems to be getting a little choked up.

I say my goodbyes on the street and tell Ms. McAllister I'll see her at O'Toole's tomorrow.

I wonder out loud why I never ran into her during my visits to Stick's place.

"Oh," she says, sighing, "Stick played it pretty close to the vest."

Driving back to the Prestwould for lunch, I think about what Terri McAllister has told me. As best I can tell, she and I spent more time with Stick Davis than anybody else over the past several months, and both of us are a bit mystified as to how Stick managed to piss somebody off enough to get himself killed, but both of us know something had him a little spooked.

Maybe Marcus Green is right. Occam's razor. Maybe, Stick being Stick, he said something insensitive to a young bandit wielding a big-boy gun.

Maybe.

❋ ❋ ❋

There isn't much to write about Stick's murder. The cops are happy with a likely suspect in jail, even if they haven't been able to find the weapon.

There is a sense of letdown in the newsroom, what with our killer hurricane spurning us. There's no point in bumping the paper up four pages now. As a matter of fact, our tiny staff might have trouble filling the Saturday rag at its present size.

"Think you can do something on the kid who killed your buddy? Like a takeout or something?" Sarah Goodnight asks hopefully.

"Allegedly killed," I correct her, "and he wasn't my buddy."

"Did you have any kind of contract with him, I mean for the rest of the money, or something in case the project didn't work out?"

"I think they call it a kill fee."

I explain about the 5K I got up front, and now that's all I'm expecting to get.

"Too bad," she says.

"Too bad his ass is dead," I reply.

"Yeah. That too."

I worry sometimes that my former mentee and present boss is getting hardened beyond her thirty-three years. There's nothing wrong with being a tough old newspaper broad, like Sally Velez, but Sarah's gone from dewy-eyed to hard-bitten in an alarmingly short period of time.

I don't think she's married to the paper, thank God. She is actually supposed to exchange vows with another human being in May, and I would be a sexist pig were I to suggest that she sweeten up a little. Still the urge is there.

I tell her that I'll see what I can cobble together for tomorrow.

"Kill fee," I hear her mutter as she walks away.

There isn't much to do except go over to the North Side and let Jerome's mother and friends tell me what an exemplary young man he is. Maybe I can even get Snake to say a kind word about the tragic passing of his brother. I already have a couple of usable quotes from Terri McAllister.

I call Marcus, who does not surprise me by telling me that he has indeed agreed to take on Sheets as his client.

"Big Boy pays promptly and well," he says, "and he owes me for keeping his butt out of prison a couple of times."

I note that I'm sure that Big Boy Sunday already has paid him dearly for that accomplishment.

"Nevertheless, he really doesn't think the kid did it. So I'm supposed to go over to the lockup tomorrow and talk to the boy."

I'm impressed. Marcus doesn't usually condescend to working on Saturdays. The pay must be good.

"Can I tag along?" I ask him.

"Yeah," he says, "I guess so. Call it your finder's fee."

I never do get over to the North Side to try to talk to Jerome's mom. All hell breaks loose outside a club in the Bottom. The odd thing is that it happened in the late afternoon. Usually you're safe over there until midnight or so, when the drunks start spilling out onto the sidewalks.

Obviously the gents who tried to make Swiss cheese out of each other were harboring grudges.

All I can get out of anybody at the scene is that two of them seemed to be accosting a third man. As is Richmond's wont, they were all armed like Rambo. When the shooting stopped, one of the two alleged assailants was dead and his partner and the other guy were hauled away by two different sets of "associates," only to show up at the emergency room separately an hour later, almost dead.

Oh, yeah. One of them (the cops didn't know who) also managed to shoot a female bartender right between the eyes when she got caught in the crossfire. Collateral damage.

So, two dead, two dying. Somebody said they thought drugs were involved.

No shit.

During Andi's bartending days, my daughter worked at this joint for six months or so. Yeah, it could have been her.

Sometimes I think we've gotten past the point that gun control could even work. The NRA has managed to turn us into Dodge City already. Maybe we ought to just arm everybody.

Sarah says they should take all the guns away from men and give every woman one.

When I mentioned that I might not be above ground now if those had been the rules back in the day, she shrugged and said something about omelets and broken eggs.

* * *

By the time I crawl between the covers sometime before one, Cindy wakes up to ask me how my evening went.

I ask her not to ask.

CHAPTER SIX

Saturday, September 7

I meet Marcus Green at his office at nine, which is about seven hours since my head hit the pillow last night.

Marcus seems a little quiet, for Marcus, as he drives us over to the city lockup.

Then he clears his throat.

"Ah, Willie, I just wanted you to be the first to know. We're expecting."

He says it like he thinks I have a vested interest in Kate's future. Hell, she always wanted kids, and her biological clock has got to be ticking like a motherfucker. I congratulate him and ask the usual questions.

"February, they say. And it's a boy. And no, we're not going to have one of those damn 'reveal' parties."

I'm surprised I didn't notice when I saw her the other day, but obliviousness was one of my many faults back when she was Kate Black.

I ask Marcus how old he is.

"What the fuck has that got to do with it?" he inquires.

"Just thinking. The boy might be the only one at his high school graduation whose daddy has to use a walker."

"I'll still be able to kick your ass in eighteen years," he replies.

I wish him luck with that and emphasize that I am pleased beyond all reason at the good news.

At the jail, we're able to see young Master Sheets after about half an hour of what I consider to be excessive suspicion on the part of the authorities.

"Do you think I've got a gun up my ass?" I ask the guy tasked with searching us.

"Don't joke about stuff like that," Marcus says.

I do recognize Jerome Sheets, although he doesn't seem to remember me. I guess all half-white guys look alike to Jerome.

He appears to weigh about 120 pounds and probably isn't more than five eight. He doesn't seem quite the modern urban gangster he fancied himself before he got himself arrested on Wednesday.

He appears, in a word, scared.

He looks like he might have been treated rudely by some of his fellow detainees, although I know that Big Boy Sunday has connections inside the lockup to ensure that nothing really unseemly happens to his charge.

"I didn't do nothing," he says when we get finally get down to the who, what, when, etc., of last Saturday night. "The door was open, and I just came in. I didn't break in or nothin'."

He tells us what he told Big Boy: Stick Davis was dead when he got there.

"Kind of freaked me out, the dude just lying there on the floor."

Not freaked out enough to keep Jerome from ransacking the place.

"You took the watch off a dead man's wrist?" I ask.

He looks at me like I'm crazy.

"He wasn't going to be usin' it no more," he explains.

Marcus just shakes his head. He and I know that his young client is facing some serious time, although Marcus has been known to work wonders with juries. The only thing hanging in the balance now is whether Jerome also killed Stick.

"I don't even have no gun," he wails. "Mr. Sunday, he don't allow that. Said I was too young."

Well, the cops haven't found one yet, not at Jerome's momma's house or anywhere else.

"Did you see any notebooks on his desk? They would have been red, like school notebooks."

He gives me a withering look.

"What the fuck I want to do with notebooks?"

Marcus tells me to go wait in the car so he can have a private chat with his new client.

When he comes back, he doesn't look confident.

"Says he didn't do it, but he admits he was in the house. Maybe the cops can pinpoint when exactly the man was killed.

"Other than that, they got the stuff he stole, they got the fingerprints. Big Boy's gonna owe me major if I get the little bastard out of this."

Then he looks over at me.

"What was all that shit about the notebooks?"

So I tell him what I didn't find.

"They let you in to snoop around?"

Quid pro quo, I explain.

"Well, damn," Marcus says. "That would be something, I suppose, if we could show that somebody took those notebooks. If we could prove that somebody else was there . . .

"But then we only have your word for it, and you're a suspect too."

I tell Marcus he's a brave man to be driving a suspected murderer around Richmond.

* * *

The goodbye party for Stick goes about as well as you'd expect for a memorial service in an Irish bar.

His brother had set it up for three in the afternoon, but many of the attendees seem to have arrived early and thirsty. I arranged with Sally to show up an hour or so late for work, and by the time I get to O'Toole's at a quarter 'til three, the place is rocking, as eternal farewell parties go.

I see a "throuple" of acquaintances from my days of running with Stick. None of them had any idea he was even back in town, but apparently somebody still reads the obit pages in our paper. Hell, I hope so. They're our main source of revenue.

There are several other people there whom I don't recognize, either friends of the deceased or kibitzers taking advantage of the snack food that I guess brother Snake sprung for, with Whit Charles's money.

A few of us exchange stories about the departed, most of which further shine his reputation as a charming asshole, with the emphasis on the noun.

"Remember the time he borrowed Freddie's car and said he'd have it back in a while . . ." one guy says.

". . . and he drove it to Daytona Beach," another mourner jumps in. "Said he just had an urge to go to the beach."

"And when Freddie finally got the car back two days later, he asked Stick why the hell he didn't just go down to Virginia Beach or the Outer Banks . . ."

"And Stick says he liked the sand better at Daytona."

Hilarity breaks out. I think I see Freddie in the crowd. He's the one who isn't laughing.

Snake is working the crowd, many of whom seem to be his friends rather than his late brother's.

Terri McAllister is there, and so is a woman of indeterminate age who claims that Stick was the love of her life before he mysteriously disappeared more than a decade ago. She says she remembers me in a way that makes me suddenly see an old friend across the room and leave her company.

"We was going to get married," she wails at one point as the stories about Stick quickly devolve into the R-rated area.

"In your fuckin' dreams," I hear Terri mutter.

I don't get much insight from the mourners, who are actually pumping me for knowledge, since they know I was the last one who admits to seeing him alive.

The man I'm waiting for shows up half an hour after I do.

Whit Charles looks pretty much like the pictures I found of him in the electronic archives. He's aged some. I know he's seventy-seven years old, and the photos I've seen are from at least fifteen years ago.

He's better dressed than most of the rest of the mob here. He and I are the only ones wearing ties. He looks like he's at least six four, and he has the wide face and square jaw of a former athlete. He has all his hair, or at least somebody's, and it's as white as a Klan rally. The hair and the glasses and an impressive tan are about the only things that seem to have changed over the last few years. His mouth is kind of turned down at the corners like his default mode is "pissed."

He looks more like a hit man than a lawyer.

Snake, who apparently only knows him via telephone from the Caribbean, goes over and shakes Charles's hand in what, for Snake, must be an unusually obsequious manner.

I slip away from another story about the deceased.

"Mr. Charles," I say as Snake is continuing to offer his undying gratitude to the man who paid for his brother's cremation and is also funding this little get-together.

He wheels around and gives me a stare that would cause lesser men to flinch.

"Who the fuck are you?" he inquires.

I explain that I'm the guy who found Stick's body.

He pushes his glasses up on his face.

"So you're the one. The ghostwriter. Hell, ghostwriter for a ghost, I guess."

I don't know how he knows that. Maybe he reads our newspaper online.

I explain the setup. I tell him that I was about half-way through the first draft when Stick was called home to Jesus.

"Hmmph," says Whit Charles. "And they think some black kid killed him? Although I hear they still haven't taken you off the suspect list."

I tell him that I have doubts about Jerome Sheets being Stick Davis's murderer.

"So that just leaves you," he says.

"Bullshit," I explain.

He looks at me for a couple of seconds hard enough that I think he might want to kick my ass.

Then he almost smiles.

"I seriously doubt that you are Stick's murderer," he says. "You don't seem like the type. I'm pretty good at first impressions."

"So who do you think did it?"

He doesn't answer at first, just looks off across the room, where it appears that one of the mourners is trying to hit on Terri McAllister, who doesn't seem to be telling him to get lost.

"I have some ideas," Charles says at last.

When I ask him for enlightenment, he looks at me again, like he's taking my measure.

"Give me your card," he says.

I dig into my wallet and can't find any. They gave us a couple of hundred each at the paper last year, but I seem to have run out. I borrow a pen and write down my cell number.

He looks at the number, then looks at me again.

"Maybe we can talk," he says. Then he turns away, headed toward the bar. End of conversation.

I hang around for a few more minutes and then leave for the office.

* * *

Never a dull moment at the house o' words.

When I get in at four thirty, there's a new rumor flying around.

Word has somehow gotten out that we soon will stop publishing on Tuesdays.

Well, that's as good a day as any. You don't want to piss off our sports enthusiasts by not having the NFL stuff in the paper Monday morning, and by Wednesday, our meager staff is already producing enough copy that we don't have to strip the wire services for content.

"Any idea whether this is bullshit or not?" I ask Sally.

She shrugs.

"Chip Grooms said he heard it from somebody he knows in advertising, and they heard it from somebody on the suits' floor."

The idea is not a new one, here or elsewhere. Better papers than ours have cut back to less than a seven-day schedule. Hell, some of them have gone from seven to zero days a week. Last thing I read said there are about 1,400 cities and towns around the country that have lost their newspapers in the past fifteen years. Pittsburgh has gone to five days a week. New Orleans. Birmingham. Mobile. The vultures are gathering.

Of course, there's always the Internet. I'm sure that if the rumors are true, I'll still be expected to post something about Monday night's mayhem online ASAP.

Nobody seems to much care that the watchdogs are being put on a very short leash. I'd be the first to admit that print journalism is not without its scoundrels and slackers, but I covered state politics for quite some time, and the politicians put our asses to shame. If we don't keep an eye on them, who the fuck will?

Wheelie is in his office with the door closed. I see that Sarah has one of the chairs across from him.

It isn't good manners, or good sense, to barge into your chief editor's office without knocking, but I flunked charm school.

"Are we really going to six days a week?" I ask them both.

Wheelie looks anxious and annoyed.

"If and when we do," he tells me, "you'll be the first to know. Now shut the door. From the outside."

I've made a living as a reporter by not taking "no" for an answer.

"I mean it," I push on. "The whole newsroom's talking about it."

Actually, there are only about ten people in the newsroom, but they do seem to be agitated.

"I know that," Wheelie says. "You think I'm deaf and blind?"

"Willie," Sarah says, "we don't know any more than you do. We've been trying to get up with B.S., but he's out of town."

Yeah, that'd be a good place for a publisher to be when the whole newsroom is in panic mode.

I don't envy either Wheelie or Sarah, who are tasked with guiding us into oblivion and having to polish this turd for our readers. Maybe we'll tell them we're cutting back to save them some time in their busy week. They won't have to waste ten minutes every Tuesday morning finding out what's going on in our fair city. And think of the trees that won't be cut down.

"Nothing's going to happen anytime soon," Wheelie says, but I can tell he's about as sure of that as I am.

I wish them luck, for all of us. It's one of those days when I kind of regret talking Sarah Goodnight into making the switch from reporter to editor.

* * *

The city is amazingly quiet for a Saturday night.

There is a police report of gunshots in a Church Hill neighborhood, but it's just some guy who locked himself out of his car and figured the best way to get in was with a pistol. They think he might have been drinking.

The cops have been catching shit for not nabbing a couple of gangs of kids who have been breaking into cars looking for loose change and whatever else the owners left inside. It turns out, according to one study a North Side neighborhood did, that the vast majority of "break-ins" did not require any breaking in at all. Car owners in our fair city are, it seems, a trusting lot. Most of the cars that were violated were not locked. A depressing number of them had items of value to fledgling criminals lying in plain sight.

"Jesus Christ," Enos Jackson says, "who leaves a cell phone in the front seat with the door unlocked in the middle of the night? Do these idiots think they're living in Mayberry?"

The blessed lull in serious crime gives me time to ponder the demise of my old buddy Stick.

Ballistic reports and common sense make it clear that he did not kill himself. Nobody shoots themselves half a dozen times, including twice in the head. That would hurt. Plus, the Stick I knew was way too selfish to have ever done something like that.

I can testify with certainty that I myself did not do the deed, even if L.D. Jones and his crack squad of chain-jerkers haven't officially removed me from the suspect list. What the hell? I was going to kill somebody who was going to give me another forty-five grand if he lived long enough to tell me the whole story?

Jerome Sheets, everybody's leading candidate, could have done the deed. He was there. He stole stuff, even Stick's treasured watch. But something just doesn't smell right about that. For one thing, Big Boy Sunday might have led me astray a time or two, but I sense that he's not lying about this, even if the kid is one of his fuck buddies' sons.

It has been my unhappy fate to talk with lots of accused felons over the years, and I think I have a pretty good nose for this kind of thing. I don't believe Jerome Sheets is capable of doing such a dastardly deed. He tried to come off as a playah while squiring Big Boy around the city, but the kid I saw in that jail cell today seemed like a small-timer who might one day grow into a stone-cold killer but hadn't nearly gotten there yet, although a few years as a guest of the state might move him in that direction.

So, I ask myself, if Jerome didn't kill Stick, who the fuck did?

I can't remember anything Stick said that might have indicated he was on somebody's to-kill list, although he was worried about something or someone. Maybe he just irritated somebody to the point of homicide.

But then I do remember something.

Strange how the mind works. You sit down and grit your teeth and try to think real hard, and the answer won't come. Then you take off your thinking cap, and it comes to you. Works for the Sunday *New York Times* crossword, and it works regarding Stick Davis too.

It hits me as I go to get a cup of newsroom coffee.

There was a night, early into my collaboration with Stick, when he brought out a bottle of bourbon. Strangely the Stickster didn't appear to be much of a drinker anymore, but this night—it must have been a Monday—he and I got into a bottle of booze and damn near killed the thing.

And as I was leaving, he told me something, something I'd since forgotten about, partly because I was drunk and partly because it didn't seem to mean anything at the time.

Stick was seeing me to the door when he stopped me and put his hand on my shoulder.

"Willie," he said, "if anything ever happens to me, you need to remember one thing: Remember the à la mode."

À la mode, not Alamo.

I thought a second or three, and then I knew what he meant.

We'd been in a joint over in the Devil's Triangle one long-ago evening, probably twenty years ago, when Stick, after a hard night of drinking, decided he wanted some dessert. Apple pie à la mode.

The waiter brought the pie out, sans ice cream. Stick made a big fuss about it.

He started berating the waiter.

"Dumbass," he said to the kid, "don't you know à la mode means with ice cream?"

Then Stick stood up and started waving his arms and yelling, "Remember the à la mode! Remember the à la mode!" And all the rest of the drunks picked up on it and started yelling too.

After that, whenever Stick had the least provocation, usually after a drink or six, he'd start yelling it to the bafflement of everyone around him.

So to humor my host that Monday night a few months ago, I told him I'd be sure to remember the à la mode.

Then he pinched down on my shoulder, causing me a surprising amount of pain.

"No shit," Stick said. "Remember. And don't forget that fuckin' horse either."

That one threw me.

"Charlestown? Forty to one?" he asked me as I slapped his hand away. He seemed incredulous that I could forget.

Then it came to me. He and I and another drunk went up to Charlestown, West Virginia, one night to play the ponies. We were down to twenty bucks among us when Stick found a hopeless long shot in the sixth race. He liked the horse because of its name: Bumpass.

"I used to date a girl from Bumpass," he told us. "Love of my life for about a month. I tell you, it's a sign."

Well, we hadn't been doing so damn well using logic, so we figured, what the hell. Win or lose, we had enough gas to get back to Richmond. So we put it all on Bumpass.

And the damn horse won. Eight hundred bucks was a lot of cash for us in those days, although I can't really tell you where it all went.

"Bumpass," he said, pronouncing it the way the natives do: BUMP-us. He made me repeat the name.

"Don't forget Bumpass either," he instructed me as I walked away in search of my car.

We never talked about either of those ridiculous artifacts from our checkered past again, but now they come back to me, even if I have no earthly idea what, if anything, Stick was talking about.

"Shouldn't you be writing something?" Sally asks. "You're just staring into space. Surely there's a dead body somewhere out there waiting to be memorialized."

I remind her that I've already done something for tomorrow's paper playing off Stick's sendoff at O'Toole's.

The piece maybe was a little less reverent than your average eulogy, but consider the source and the setting.

"I've got nothing," I inform my most immediate editor.

Two games of solitaire later, I call it a night, still thinking about ice cream and an overachieving horse.

CHAPTER SEVEN

Sunday, September 8

Some of the waitresses at Joe's have more patience than others. The one today is not inclined to suffer fools gladly if at all.

R.P. McGonnigal insists on interrogating her about the biscuits.

"Are they really fluffy today?" he asks.

We've already been here forty-five minutes and have put her off once on ordering anything more nourishing than cheap Bloody Marys.

She seems undisposed to cheerfully put up with such nonsense. She stares at him for a moment, pencil and pad in hand.

"They're about as fluffy as they ever are," she answers at last. It is a fair assessment. The biscuits at Joe's, while second to none in their bulk, tend to be a bit on the chewy side.

"They are biscuits with substance," Andy Peroni once said in an apt and kind defense.

It is obvious that the next thing the waitress wants to hear from R.P. is his order.

Not to be.

"Do you think," R.P. presses on, "you could ask the cook to make me one that's especially fluffy. I'm really in the mood for something fluffy today."

She puts the pencil and pad back in her pocket.

"I'll check back later," she says between clenched teeth as she walks away.

"God damn, R.P.," Cindy says, "I'm getting hungry. Stop fucking with the waitress."

R.P.'s friend, a guy who's a nurse over at VCU Hospitals and hasn't been here before, asks him what's the deal with fluffy biscuits.

"You can get a fluffy biscuit at Hardee's, for shit's sake."

"Ah," R.P. says, "but you can't get this kind of ambience."

Abe walks over and has a few words with the aggrieved waitress.

"She'll be back in a minute," he informs us when he returns. "She'd like to take our orders then."

"What did you say to her?" Andy Peroni's wife asks. Ms. Peroni, the former Grace Biggers of the Cherry Street Biggerses, sits next to her husband. She is making a rare appearance at our Sunday morning brunch fest. She and Andy have split and gotten back together at least three times. Cindy, being Andy's sister, is not one of her biggest fans. We have managed to seat them outside clawing reach.

Abe shrugs.

"I just told her the guy asking about the biscuits wasn't quite right, and she shouldn't pay him any attention."

R.P. takes umbrage at this, but when our schoolmarm of a waitress comes back, he meekly orders the same damn thing he's been ordering for twenty years, including a biscuit that most certainly won't be specially prepared for him, unless the waitress spits on it.

R.P., Andy, Mrs. Andy, and R.P.'s friend all want to know the latest on Stick Davis.

"It's kind of exciting," Andy says, "sitting next to a suspected murderer."

"He's killed before, and he might kill again," Cindy says to her brother.

I tell them most of what I know. They wouldn't have to ask me if they'd read the paper, which I suspect none of them are doing these days.

"So this black kid, you think he maybe didn't do it?" R.P.'s friend asks. "Seems like him doing the deed takes the heat off you."

Yeah, I explain, but if he's actually not guilty, convicting him would kind of suck.

"How about the fella that paid for the funeral? Charles something? He came all the way up here from the islands for the funeral. What's his story?"

"Well, Stick was his employee," R.P. says. "Maybe he just felt bad about him getting killed."

Cindy stares at him.

"You did know Stick, right?" she asks.

He nods his head. He, Abe, Andy, and Mrs. Andy remember Stick from the old days, when they got to know him through me, and Cindy's heard all the stories.

"Well, everybody's got somebody that cares about them," R.P. says.

"Allegedly," Cindy amends.

"What was he doing down there all that time?" Abe asks. Even though he lives with me and Cindy, we haven't talked much about Stick's book. I didn't want to talk about it until it was done, and Abe isn't much for interrogating.

I tell them what I know from what the deceased revealed to me, leaving out some of the spicier and perhaps felonious escapades.

"And he didn't leave any notes or anything?"

So I tell them about the missing notebooks.

"Man," Andy says, "this shit is getting deep."

My old Oregon Hill buds are in agreement that it doesn't make any sense that the kid who stole Stick's watch and other items of value would have absconded with a bunch of notebooks.

"Must be some good shit in there," says Grace Peroni. "I mean, worth killing for, you know?"

Maybe, I concede.

I agree with them that it would be a good idea to have a further conversation with Whit Charles.

"How was the biscuit?" Andy asks R.P. as we're getting ready to leave about an hour after the waitress wished us to do so.

R.P. says it definitely was not fluffy.

* * *

Abe is going over to Stella Stellar's apartment, where he'll probably spend the afternoon and perhaps the night. She and the redoubtable Goldfish Crackers are back from a tour, if gigs in Danville, Wytheville, and some place in east Tennessee can be called a tour.

Cindy and I get back a little after one. We're walking into the lobby when my cell phone vibrates in my pocket. I check the number. Big Boy Sunday.

"What's going on, Willie?"

I assume he's inquiring about the status of Jerome Sheets.

I fill him in on the visit Marcus and I paid to the kid yesterday, noting that Jerome seemed to be a little out of his element in the lockup.

"Well," Big Boy says, "I got some folks there looking out for him."

The man has connections on both sides of the bars. I don't really want to know which cops are beholden to him.

"What'd you think?" he asks.

"About what?"

"About whether you think my boy's a killer or not."

I tell Big Boy that I've been fooled more than once on that score. Hell, everybody says they're innocent until it's proved that they're not.

"But, no, he didn't seem like the kind of kid who'd shoot somebody seven or eight times over a watch."

"Thass what I've been telling you," he says. "You think that lawyer, that Marcus Green, can get him off?"

I explain that Jerome surely will be doing some time for stealing a dead man's possessions, but that if anybody can get him free of a murder rap, it's Marcus.

"Maybe he can get him sentenced as a juvie," Big Boy says. "The boy ain't but seventeen."

It is possible, I concede.

"His momma's been on my ass about this. She wants the boy home."

Big Boy probably has been a driving force in the boy's life, no doubt introducing him to a world where people steal dead men's stuff. I resist mentioning that to him.

I am puzzled, though, at the big man's interest in Jerome. Hell, he must see one of his junior henchmen sent up for this and that on occasion.

I ask Big Boy how long he and Jerome's mother have been friendly with each other.

He hesitates, then says he reckons about twenty years.

"That's a long time. Long enough to see a kid grow up."

"Willie," he says, "you don't need to know every damn thing. Just make sure that lawyer gets the boy off."

I'm thinking that maybe Marcus Green ought to know whose kid he's representing. It might inspire him to try harder.

* * *

I've just dozed off watching the Redskins-Eagles game when the phone interrupts my Sunday peace again.

"We need to talk."

I don't recognize the voice and am getting ready to hang up when he says, "You're that nosy-ass reporter, right? The one from the memorial for Stick?"

I mute the TV and motion for Cindy to bring me a notepad and a pen.

"Mr. Charles, I presume."

"I'd just as soon you didn't say my name."

"You said we need to talk."

"Yeah," my caller replies. "You think you know what's what, but you don't. I'd like to set the record straight."

I ask if he'd like to drop by the Prestwould and discuss it further.

He laughs and says he doesn't think so.

"I'd rather we met somewhere, let's say neutral. And it has to be off the record, at least for now."

You take your leads where you can get 'em. When he suggests a commuter parking lot halfway to Charlottesville, how can I refuse?

"No recording devices," Charles stipulates. "And no damn photos either. This is background."

So I make myself a quick cup of coffee on the new gadget Cindy convinced me we really needed, a machine so simple even I can usually operate it. I tell my beloved I'm off to a secret meeting.

"Male or female?" she inquires.

I tell her I'll be back soon.

On the way out on I-64, I ponder just what the fuck Whit Charles might want to tell me. I know he's a lawyer. I know he is, by all accounts, a shady lawyer, one who might have done time if he wasn't by profession an expert in gaming the system. Those electronic news clippings from his days "managing" his clients' money attest to that.

From what I've learned ghostwriting the first half of Stick Davis's biography, I suspect Charles didn't suddenly find Jesus after he beat a hasty retreat to the Caribbean.

And I wonder if the second part of Stick's story, the part in those lost notebooks, didn't present a very real threat to his employer.

So why pay for Stick's burial expenses and come to the wake? And how did he even know he was dead?

The commuter parking lot is nearly empty, this being a Sunday. I see a big-ass Denali sitting at the far end of the lot. Its driver blinks the lights.

The thing's so huge I might need a footstool to get inside. I'm reminded of Cindy's remark once, when one of these gas gluttons was blotting out the sun next to us at a stoplight.

"Jesus," she said, "the assholes who make these things would probably like to turn Denali into an oil refinery."

Charles is sitting behind the wheel. The air conditioning is on high.

"Before you get in," he says, stopping me at the door, "Gino wants to make sure you're not recording this."

And then I see that there's another guy in the Denali. Gino, who looks to be a native of the islands, slides out of the back seat, hops to the pavement, and asks me to spread my arms.

I ask if he's from TSA. He doesn't speak and doesn't smile, just pats me down, takes my cell phone and then nods up at his boss. If I patted him down, I'd lay odds he'd be a lot better armed than me.

"Don't worry," the lawyer says. "Gino won't hurt you. I just want a witness to all this, and no record of it. Insurance, if you will."

I lie and tell him that my wife knows where I am and who I'm meeting. My insurance.

Gino, it turns out, is an Italian by birth who decided for whatever reasons to spend the rest of his life in the islands.

"What do you want to know?" Charles asks me.

There's no sense in pussyfooting around. I'm out here in a deserted parking lot with a guy who's been known to at least bend the rules.

"Did you kill Stick Davis, or have him killed?"

He is taken aback for a moment, and then he laughs, as does his back-seat buddy.

"Yeah," he says. "I thought you might be thinking along those lines. That's the main reason I wanted you out here. To straighten things out."

I wait for more. I figure that Charles, a trained ambulance chaser, knows the value of silence when trying to get a witness or interviewee to open up, but he obviously has something to tell me.

"OK," he says at last, "here's how it is."

And he tells me more about Stick Davis's decade in Virgin Gorda than Stick himself ever did. Assuming, of course, that he's telling the truth.

"Stick was quite a character," he says. "He wasn't a half-bad cook, and he was willing to do whatever needed to be done."

From what Stick hinted, I had been pretty sure "whatever" involved something dicier than whipping up an omelet at midnight.

There were, Charles says, some "shipments" that needed to be picked up and delivered. He explains that the island doesn't have a big town of any sort "just a lot of coves and little harbors."

"I think Stick found his niche down there," Charles says. "As you might know, he was not a man of tedious moral restrictions. He knew how the world works."

He says that he was genuinely sorry when Stick left the islands "in rather a hurry" and that he was somewhat devastated to find out about his "untimely demise."

I ask him how he knew all about that.

Charles takes his glasses off and wipes them on his shirt.

"Oh," he says, "I keep an eye on things. I wanted to know what was going on with Mr. Davis. At some point, he and I were going to have to have a meeting."

And then he tells me the real reason he had kept such an interest in Stick after he left Virgin Gorda.

"There was a safe," he begins.

The safe contained quite a bit of currency that wasn't ever going to show up on anybody's tax returns. Stick managed to get the combination.

"It was stupid of me, really," Charles says. "I had a security camera in the room where the safe was. All someone, and it had to have been Stick, had to do was look at the video later. When I opened the safe, I suppose the camera recorded my movements."

Stick Davis was already back in the States by the time Whit Charles realized his stash was about one hundred thousand dollars short.

"I knew he'd been taking a little here and there, maybe selling some of the product on his own, but it was small potatoes, although I guess it added up over time.

"The thing is, Mr. Black, the islands are not a place for the pure of heart. A little larceny is what you expect instead of income taxes down there. And it's a lot less expensive."

I hear Gino chuckle.

"But the theft from my safe offended me. I had treated Stick like a son. Well, like a red-headed stepson, but still, it was unkind of him, don't you think?"

I nod.

"I never intended to do him any real harm, and I never did," Charles goes on, "but I made it clear to him that I knew where he was and what he had done. He knew he couldn't escape me, and he promised that someday soon he would return to the island and repay me."

I note that, to an impartial observer, he still looks like a prime candidate for the murder of Stick Davis.

"As do you, Mr. Black. I understand he had promised you another, what, forty-five thousand when this book was finished. My forty-five thousand, by the way."

It would be rude and dumb of me to tell him that, considering our comparative histories, he's more likely to have shot somebody a few times over monetary differences than I am.

I ask the most obvious question.

"If you didn't kill him, and I didn't kill him, and that kid in the city lockup didn't do it, then who did?"

Charles clears his throat.

"I have a theory," he says.

Tell me, I implore.

"All in good time, Mr. Black. All in good time."

We're both silent for a moment.

"By the way," he continues, "you didn't happen to take anything from the scene of the crime, did you?"

I assure him that I did not, that I was under the watchful eye of Richmond's finest when I was allowed in.

"Yes," he says, "but no one was watching when you found him dead, were they?"

I know where he's going with this. He has to know that Stick had something of value in his study, something that wasn't there later.

"I knew he had some notebooks," I tell Charles, "but they weren't there when I was let back in. And the kid who's in jail most likely didn't take them. Why would he?"

"That's a shame," he says. "I don't think it will shock you to learn that whoever took those notebooks probably took poor Mr. Davis's life as well."

Yes, I tell him, the thought had occurred to me.

"I know you probably think it was me, with everything he probably told you, or at least hinted at, about our business relationship, but trust me, Mr. Black, there is something else going on here, something beyond you and me."

"Trust me" is one of those phrases that activate my bullshit detector. People often say it, and other giveaways like "honestly" or "I'll tell you the truth," when they're lying like dogs. However, sometimes "trust me" means trust me. I'll go with face value for now.

I indicate that my ears are all his on the matter of who he thinks might have killed Stick Davis.

"Later," Whit Charles says. "First, though, I have to check on something."

When I ask him where he's living during his brief return to the commonwealth, he says he has a place he's staying in the West End. I ask him if he can be more specific.

"I could," he says, "but I won't."

He leaves it at that and reiterates that our conversation never happened. I can only agree with him.

Gino, he explains, knows where I live.

❋ ❋ ❋

By the time I get home, the Skins have lost another one.

"Maybe they should change their name," Cindy suggests.

It has been suggested, I reply.

"By the way, that girl, Sarah, called. She said it was important."

Cindy has some inkling that Sarah Goodnight and I might have done a sleepover long ago. Or maybe she is just hostile to attractive younger women in general. She certainly gives off that vibe when it comes to Sarah.

I remind her that "that girl" is one of my bosses.

"Whatever," my beloved says.

Sarah is at home when I call.

"I'm sorry to disturb your day of rest," she says. Her voice sounds a little shaky.

I tell her never mind, my day of rest has already been shot to hell.

"I'm kind of worried," Sarah continues.

Sarah isn't one to worry much, or at least to admit it if she does.

"Girls can't be pussies," she explained to me once.

"Tell me what's wrong."

What's wrong is Luther Gates.

He owns a group of furniture stores around the state. It's been a family business for three generations. It seems to be thriving, but Luther's future is somewhat in doubt at present because he allegedly made a trip to Culpeper recently to meet a female he had met online.

There were, according to the story we ran last Wednesday, three problems. One, Luther is married. Two, the female told him she was thirteen years old. Three, "she" wasn't a female but rather an enterprising state trooper who handcuffed him and took him away to jail when he showed up with candy and flowers.

Three strikes and you're out. Or, in Luther's case, maybe in the big house for quite some time.

He is free, somehow, on sizable bond, and from what Sarah is telling me, he probably shouldn't be.

"He's crazy," she says. "He blames me for everything. He said I've ruined his life."

As it turns out, Luther, upon being arrested and then released on bond, called the paper to beg us not to use his name. Chuck Apple, who was working the story, passed the buck up the ladder to Sarah, who was our adult supervision in the newsroom that day.

"I told him we would run whatever the police gave us, and he just went nuts. He said we were destroying him and his family. I told him that he seemed to have done that pretty much by himself. Maybe I was a little insensitive."

I offer that little sensitivity should have been proffered to a fifty-something guy who was hoping to bang a middle-school girl he'd never met. Even with my sorry record, I've never since the age of twenty-one done the nasty with a woman who wasn't old enough to vote.

"Anyhow, he said if his name was in the paper, he couldn't be responsible for what happened."

"Did you call the cops?" I ask.

No, she didn't.

"I figured he was just having a panic attack and that he'd realize we weren't his problem."

The story ran, complete with a photo of Luther Gates doing the walk of shame with a cheap sports jacket over his head.

"And then Jack and I got back in town this afternoon from a weekend in the mountains, and there was Grover, lying in the backyard."

She's crying now. Grover is Sarah and her live-in fiancé's beagle. Or, rather, was. The girl who fed him and walked him yesterday said he was fine when she left about eight last night.

"His throat was cut," she says, between sobs. "Who the hell would do that?"

She knows though. There was a note on the coffee table.

"I warned you," was all it said.

"He broke into our damn house, and he killed my dog. Oh, and he crapped on the carpet."

Jack has called the cops already, but they haven't gotten back to him yet. Sarah thought I might be able to find out something, like whether they've arrested the son of a bitch again.

I get up with L.D. Jones at home. He confirms what I kind of feared.

Luther Gates, alleged child molester and suspected dog murderer and carpet despoiler, is in the wind.

Sarah does not seem pleased by this news.

"Do you still have a gun?" I ask, fondly remembering the time she saved my ass by shooting a man intent on ending my stay on Earth.

"Oh, hell yeah."

"So," Cindy says when I come back into the living room, "tell me all about your day of rest."

CHAPTER EIGHT

Monday, September 9

My second consecutive "off" day turns out to be no less restful than the first.

Cindy's out molding young minds, and the thought of spending a few hours alone with Butterball, my step-cat who lives up to her name more and more by the day, seems less than appealing. So, after a couple of cups of coffee, I vacate the premises.

It's a fine late-summer day, not too hot or too cold for me to walk across Monroe Park and then over the Downtown Expressway to Oregon Hill, a two-Camel walk.

Peggy and Awesome Dude are watching one of the shopping channels. They're biding their time until *The Price Is Right*, the high point of their morning educational stimulation, comes on.

There is no use in pointing out to my mother and her live-in friend that they probably are losing brain cells watching this crap. I suppose it is more entertaining if you're stoned.

I did mention my concerns once.

"Hard words," Peggy replied, not taking her eyes off some idiot in a clown suit having an orgasm over being chosen to make a fool of herself in front of millions, "from a man who spends perfectly good Sunday afternoons watching the Washington Redskins."

Touché.

Awesome wants to know the latest about "that guy you were supposed to of killed."

I tell them enough to assuage their fears that I might be spending the rest of my life in prison, not mentioning that I still don't have the official clean bill of health from L.D. Jones's stalwart posse.

"Well," Awesome says, "just be sure you got a good lawyer. I seen this guy the other day on *Law and Order* . . ."

The only way to really engage in a long, meaningful conversation with the Dude is to take a couple of tokes, and I've got things I'd like to do this morning that require having my meager wits about me.

Peggy catches me up on the latest news about my daughter and grandson. Andi and Walter see my old mom more than they see me, which is my bad as much as theirs.

When the formerly fat host comes blasting onto the screen urging us all to "come on down," it's time to leave.

This seems like a good morning to make another visit to the general vicinity of Jordan's Branch to see if I can engage any of Stick Davis's former neighbors. I walk back to the Prestwould, get in the venerable Honda, and head west.

Taking a right off Patterson onto Glenburnie, I drive past the church and take another right on Stokes Lane. I see the modest one-story house Stick was renting up ahead on the left. It no long appears to be an active crime scene.

What I'd like to know is whether any of Stick's neighbors can tell me anything about him. In the time we spent together working on the book, I don't recall him mentioning any of them, and no one came by while I was there.

I see a rather substantial black lady watching me through her screen door in the house beside Stick's. I go over and introduce myself.

Mrs. Woolfolk doesn't seem to want to talk to me at first, but when she realizes I'm a harmless reporter, she opens up a little.

"You got to be careful around here," she says. "I'm part of the neighborhood watch."

Yeah, the fact that guys like Jerome Sheets might just wander through your neighborhood looking for an unlocked door should make people more watchful.

"No, he didn't have nothing much to say," the lady tells me when I ask about Stick. "He just kept to himself. Didn't hurt nobody. Sure didn't deserve what he got."

Before I leave to go knock on some more doors, I ask her if she knew anything about the break-in.

"No," she says, "but there was them other guys, the ones that must of come later."

I stop.

"Other guys?"

"The paper said that boy broke into the house on a Saturday night, but this was on Sunday. I know because I was getting ready to go to Sunday night services."

What Mrs. Woolfolk says she saw was a couple of guys parking in front of Stick's house.

"They went in, and then they come out again, and they had some stuff. They come in with like a grocery bag, but it looked empty, and it was full when they come out."

"Like maybe notebooks?"

"I couldn't tell. It was in that bag."

I ask her if she had told the police about the men.

"No. I figured they was friends or something. And the police didn't never talk to me," she says. "And it didn't seem to matter much at the time. But now, thinking about them going in there and him already dead, it does seem peculiar."

To say the least.

I guess that, once the police got their man, or boy, the hapless Jerome Sheets, they didn't much care about canvassing the neighborhood.

Mrs. Woolfolk doesn't remember much about what the two guys looked like.

"Just a couple of kind of mean-looking white boys. They was either bald or had shaved their heads. And, oh, I think one of them had a tattoo on his forehead."

"His forehead?"

"Yeah. I couldn't make it out, but I'm pretty sure that's what it was."

They were driving "some kind of dark-colored van."

When I've milked Mrs. Woolfolk dry, I thank her.

On my way out, she says, "You know, you look familiar. Did you ever know a fella named Richard Slade?"

We're cousins, I tell her.

"My land. Well, I thought so. I went to school with him. That was terrible, what they did, sending him to prison for something he didn't do. And then trying to put him back in again."

There's no sense in my mentioning my role in once saving Richard Slade's ass. I have that fancy three-dollar Virginia Press Association award for my role in it. Reward enough for anyone.

* * *

I HAVE an address for Terri McAllister. Having no better way to piss away an off day, I stop by unannounced.

She lives in a place near the Downtown Expressway, a little north of Carytown. When she answers the door, she seems less than thrilled to see me.

"I got to be at work in forty-five minutes," she says.

I assure her that I won't take up that much of her time.

She opens the screen door. I start to squash out my smoke. She says, "Hell, don't worry about that. You could probably get cancer from licking the damn walls in here."

She doesn't ask me to sit, and she doesn't either, making it clear that the clock is ticking.

I tell her what Stick's next-door neighbor told me about the two men who "visited" his place, apparently more than a day after his demise.

"Did you ever hear him say anything about any problems, about anybody that was, um, unhappy with him about anything?"

She laughs, with damn little humor.

"You asked me about that the other day. Stick probably made a lot of people unhappy, from some of the stories they were telling at O'Toole's. But I don't know that he had made anybody mad enough to kill him."

"Did he ever seem like he was worried, like he was looking over his shoulder or something?"

She looks at her watch and sighs.

"Not that I can recall. He was a little jumpy, but I figured that was just him. You didn't want to slip up on him all of a sudden. Sometimes I'd accidentally wake him up, and he'd go all Kung-Fu until he realized it was just me. So somebody came in after he was killed, and they just left and took something of his?"

"That's what the lady said it looked like."

I mention the notebooks that I couldn't find.

"Damn," says Terri McAllister, putting out her cigarette in the sink. "Sounds like ol' Stick was keeping a few secrets from me."

Welcome to the club, I tell her.

She promises to call me if she thinks of anything else.

❊ ❊ ❊

NEXT STOP is police headquarters.

L.D. Jones is delighted to spare me a few minutes. Kidding. But when I relay the message through his pit-bull administrative aide that I have information about the Stick Davis case, I am granted a brief audience.

"Why," the chief asks, "are you bothering me? You ought to be glad we found someone who's a more likely suspect than you."

I assure L.D. that I do not relish crapping on his parade, but that I have information I'm sure he'll want me to share.

"Just doing my civic duty."

The chief makes a rude sound. When I tell him about Mrs. Woolfolk and the visitors the late Stick had between Jerome's visit and my discovering his corpse, he tries not to appear interested.

"I'm sure your detectives must have interviewed her," I add, "her living right next door and all, but I guess the lady has a bad memory, because she doesn't recall talking to the police."

L.D. shakes his head.

"She might have been mistaken about the day," he says finally, hopefully.

I burst his bubble by telling him how the lady knew they came by on Sunday.

"Well," the chief says, "who knows what they wanted? But we've still got the killer locked up here. He broke in, walked in, whatever, on Saturday and when we catch him, he tells us right off that there was a dead guy there but he didn't kill him, just worked around him. You believe that, and I've some land just off Virginia Beach I'd like to sell you."

I suggest that the men who dropped by late Sunday afternoon might have had a horse in this race.

"Like what?"

If I knew that, I tell L.D., I'd have a lot better idea why my old buddy Stick's ashes are sitting in a box in his brother's living room.

"I'm just saying," I add, "that there's something going on here that goes beyond some dickhead kid killing a guy in a robbery gone bad."

I haven't brought Whit Charles's name into my conversations with the chief, at least not yet. No sense in muddying the waters. Especially since Gino knows where I live.

I'm not inclined to think Charles murdered his former employee. He's probably committed plenty of offenses worthy of incarceration, but there's something else going on here, Stick-wise, and if I bide my time a bit, Mr. Charles might show me the light.

"You know what your problem is?" the chief asks, and proceeds to tell me. "You've got too much imagination."

And you don't have enough, the thought balloon over my head reads. Hell, I know that Occam and his fucking razor are usually right, that the simplest answer is the right one, but for our city's finest, the original simple answer to who killed Stick Davis was yours truly. Is it possible that the cops have whiffed on this second "simple answer" as well?

❊ ❊ ❊

After a late, two-beer lunch at Perly's, I stop by the office. Might as well completely butcher my day off, and Cindy won't be home for another couple of hours at least.

I want to check in with Sarah, to see if the bastard who killed her dog has been caught yet. When I walk into the newsroom, though, it's obvious that my boss and former protégé is not the only one having issues today.

I smell layoffs.

I catch a whiff of panic when I step off the elevator. You come to recognize it after it's happened five or six times, which it has with our ill-used staff over the past few years.

People are gathered in little clusters, speaking low, trying not to draw attention to themselves. A young photographer breaks the silence by loudly stating the obvious: "This sucks."

I walk into Sarah's office.

"Who?"

She motions for me to shut the door, although it's obvious that whatever bad news she possesses is already public knowledge.

It has occurred to me, as it always does at times like this, that this time the "who?" might be me. God knows I've made enough enemies. And my salary, just enough to pay the rent, groceries, cigarettes, and beer, with a little left to put into the 401(k), is huge compared with what newbies like Leighton Byrd and Callie Ann Boatwright are making.

When Sarah tells me about the assistant state editor, two reporters, and a photographer who no longer work here, I feel really badly for them but also realize that I have started breathing again. I am learning to live with survivor's guilt.

She concurs with the kid photographer. This really does suck. Nobody can figure a way to get anyone under the age of forty to subscribe to a damn print newspaper, and nobody wants to pay shit for an online publication that they used to get for free. All the advertising we get is paid obits, going-away presents from the families of our dearly departed readers.

They've gotten rid of two guys in advertising, too, and a circulation manager.

"What have I gotten myself into?" Sarah mutters, loud enough for me to hear.

I assure her that, when and if her own judgment day comes, she has the chops and the résumé to land on her feet somewhere else.

"Like cranking out bullshit for a health-care company? Or maybe I could shill for Big Tobacco. In the meantime, I get to fuck up good people's lives."

She says that, just between me and her, she has been testing the waters with some of the online news sites.

"It's the future, Willie," she says.

Not for me, I assure her.

"Well," she says, "no offense, but I've got a hell of a lot more future to worry about than you do."

Ouch.

"Speaking of fucking up people's lives," I ask, "what about Luther Gates?"

"No change. The cops are looking for him, but they don't know where he is. His soon-to-be-ex-wife says she hasn't heard from him and doesn't expect to."

"You're still armed?"

She gives me a tight little smile.

"Yeah. In my purse. The guards downstairs know about it, and so does B.S."

"Well," I say, speaking from experience, "you know how to use it. Just be careful."

"I kind of wish the son of a bitch would confront me or something. Right now, I'm in the mood to shoot somebody. Especially after what he did to Grover."

I tell her that, on the bright side, I might have a pretty good story for our flagging rag, but that it might take a couple more days to flesh out.

"Tell me," she says. "Take my mind off all this shit."

I follow her gaze out into the newsroom, where four compatriots are gathered around the assistant editor, a woman who has been here almost as long as I have, is divorced, and has a grown daughter with health issues living with her.

"Wheelie and I had to make the decisions," Sarah says. "We had to have one less editor. If it wasn't Ruth, the other possibility was Reed, the guy who has to take off every Tuesday for chemo."

That does, I concur, suck.

I tell her most of what I know about Stick Davis's possible assassin or assassins. Kid comes in to rob the place Saturday night and finds a dead body but doesn't tell anyone. A couple of goons show up late Sunday afternoon and leave with a grocery bag full of something or other. I find Stick's body on Monday and get put on the L.D. Jones Most Wanted list, soon to be supplanted by the feckless Jerome Sheets. I manage to get back inside for a quick look and I can't find the one thing I really wanted to find: Stick's notebooks.

Sarah sighs and shakes her head.

"You've written most of that already, except the part about the two guys on Sunday. Give me something new."

And so I tell her about my little meeting with Whit Charles, without mentioning his name just yet.

"So this guy, he was Davis's boss down there in, what, Virgin Gordo?"

"Gorda. Yeah."

"And he thinks somebody else wanted Stick dead, somebody other than you and the kid? But what about this guy? From what you're telling me, it seems like he had as good a reason as any to kill him."

I tell her that I don't believe he did it.

"Why not?"

"For one thing, he came back here for the memorial. He's made himself pretty visible. He even paid the burial expenses. He met with me and told me, about Stick stealing his money and all."

"And you can write this?"

Not just yet, I tell her. I did make some promises that professional standards and concern for my health make it essential that I keep.

"But he's going to tell me more."

"When?"

Soon, I tell her, not adding "I hope."

* * *

I WALK over to one of the little clumps of my peers who are wishing good luck to a woman who is going to need it.

Wheelie, our top editor, has come down from a meeting with the suits and is walking over to offer his condolences, a brave gesture, I have to admit, from a man who helped choose her as our latest sacrifice to the gods of the Grimm Group, our corporate masters.

Ruth says nothing when he tells her what anyone with any guts or common decency would tell the person he's just fired. He offers assurances that she was a fine editor who didn't do anything wrong except be in this godforsaken business at the wrong time, that everything will somehow be all right. He promises to help her find another job at the tender age of fifty-seven and "land on her feet."

Ruth and Wheelie and the rest of us, who are looking down and trying to will ourselves to disappear from this embarrassing scene, know it's all bullshit, but Wheelie's trying.

Ruth doesn't curse him or spit in his face. She just looks at him, nods her head, turns, and walks toward the elevators.

Wheelie and I exchange glances. The others go their separate ways. Nobody says anything to Wheelie, probably for fear that any negative attention might put them at the top of our dwindling list of working journalists.

Our boss looks at me as he walks past.

"I need a drink," says Wheelie, who doesn't drink.

CHAPTER NINE

Tuesday, September 10

For the first time since I found Stick Davis's body, I take a look at the half-done manuscript I've saved on my home computer screen. It's quiet in our apartment, with Cindy off to school and Butterball taking her post-breakfast nap, which will last until the next feeding time. Lying there basking in the sun coming in the living-room windows, the animal almost looks like acceptable company.

Stick's biography isn't the most boring thing I've ever written or read, with plenty of salacious and/or criminal content. However, as it reads now, it wasn't going to make Stick much, if any, money or win me the Pulitzer Prize for nonfiction.

Was Stick feeding me a line about holy-shit secrets to come? I wonder if I'll ever know.

There is one thing, though, that gets my attention. I didn't pay it much mind when he mentioned it. I find it where I stuck it, halfway through the seventh chapter.

"There were guys down there," I quote him as saying, "who were kind of scary. Some of the things they told me made me realize that all the nuts aren't back in the States. Some of them went south."

And that's it. His narrative moves on to his latest underage island girl conquest. He said he'd talk about the aforementioned nuts later.

I speed-read the deathless prose I wrote before Stick left us and don't learn anything else, except maybe I shouldn't quit the day job to write books. I'm better at the stuff you line your birdcage with the next morning.

I'm on my third cup of coffee when my phone rings.

It's Terri McAllister.

"I remembered something," she says. "It might not be anything, but I thought you'd want to know."

What Terri remembered is an iPad.

"I thought about what you said about the missing notebooks, and it made me think. Stick had an iPad. He had it with him last time I saw him, and he was always writing shit on it. And you said there wasn't anything like that when you went back and looked later?"

I answer in the negative. Now that Terri mentions it, I do remember seeing it there on the table once or twice. I even saw Stick pick it up once and tap something into it.

"Like I said, it might not be nothing, but you asked me to call you if I remembered anything."

I thank her profusely and promise to take her to dinner soon, somewhere better than that greasy spoon where she works.

"Aw, cut the bullshit," Terri says. "I just thought this might help."

I call L.D. Jones's office. After being frozen out by his unhelpful aide, despite my assertion that I have a hot tip about the Stick Davis murder, I give up and do something I try not to do if I can help it. I text Peachy Love and ask her to call me when and if she can do it without drawing suspicion.

Five minutes later, she calls me.

"This better be good," my former journalism compatriot and present police flack says. "The chief is watching my ass lately, like he thinks I might be consorting with the enemy."

She's stepped out of the building for a minute. I assure her that I'd never call her or text her at work if it wasn't a big deal.

"No," she says when I ask, "I never heard anybody say anything about finding an iPad or anything like that. Doesn't sound like something we'd try to keep secret. I know they seized his desk-top computer, but they didn't find anything interesting on it, from what I hear."

I thank her and let her get back inside. As with Terri McAllister, I tell her that I owe her one. Like Terri, she tells me to cut the bullshit. I guess I need to work on my sincerity.

So Stick had an iPad and it wasn't there when the cops and I snooped around later. Hell, lots of people have iPads. There isn't any real reason to think that he had stored stuff away on his that he didn't want anyone to see.

Still, the fact that he had one, and neither the cops nor I saw it, makes me wonder. Maybe the guys who came by for a "visit" that Sunday took it.

But another thought occurs to me. It seems like an iPad might be just the kind of thing a small-time dickhead kid crook might snatch while he was robbing a dead man's house.

I think about getting Jerome Sheets's mother's address, either from the cops or Big Boy Sunday, but then I have a better idea.

Marcus Green answers his own phone. I cut to the chase and ask him if his junior felon client mentioned anything to him about picking up an iPad while he was rummaging through Stick's apartment.

"Nah. I think when they caught him they got everything he took. Why?"

I tell Marcus about the iPad. I point out to him that, if the boy did take the iPad and has it cached away at his momma's or somewhere else, it might be good if he told us, since there might be something on there that could get his ass out of the major crack it's in right now.

"Yeah," Marcus says. "I have to talk to the dummy this afternoon about his defense, such as it is. I'll find out what I can. So you say the cops don't have it?"

"That's what my source tells me."

"Well," he says, "Peachy ought to know."

I wonder how Marcus knows about Peachy and hope he's in a minority of one.

After that, I call Whit Charles, hoping that he might be willing and able to tell me anything else about whatever he hinted at on Sunday.

I leave a message, and he calls me back five minutes later.

I read him the one paragraph in the manuscript where Stick alluded to "scary guys" from the States who went "down south."

He's silent for a few seconds.

"Yeah," he says finally, "that sounds about right."

There's a pause. I hear him clear his throat.

"We need to talk somewhere else. Somewhere private."

I ask him if he thinks his phone's tapped or something. He just tells me that he'll call me back later. Then he hangs up.

* * *

Andi gives me a call. She has a day off today and asks if I want to meet her for coffee. William's in kindergarten, Walter's at work.

"Just us."

I've had my day's worth of caffeine already but don't want to pass up a chance to spend some time, quality or otherwise, with my only offspring.

We meet at one of the coffee shops in Carytown. Andi lives pretty close to a Starbucks but wants to support local businesses, plus they skin you a little less thoroughly for a cup of java than Fourbucks does.

Andi has put on a pound or two but is still definitely ahead of the curve for a thirty-year-old with a kid. Her hair's copper-colored these days. She seems to be thriving, happy with her roles as mother, wife, and social worker.

"So," she says, "are you in the clear now?"

I give her the *Cliff's Notes* version of the Stick Davis affair as it stands so far.

She says she'd really like me to get to know her Walter better. I tell her that he's aces in my book because he's good to her.

"About time somebody treated you like you deserve."

She seems to know that I'm talking about my history as a piss-poor father.

"Ah," she says, waving my words away, "you did the best you could."

Not true, but sometimes it's best to just shut up.

After we've hogged the place for an hour or so, no doubt depriving a fledgling novelist of a nook in which to park his ass for half a day with his muse, my phone buzzes.

It's Whit Charles.

He sounds like he's in a car somewhere.

"Do you know where Zion Crossroads is off I-64?" he asks.

I know the exit, I assure him.

"You need to get out here," he says. He gives me directions to a place that's a couple of turns off the interstate and says I should drive there as quick as I can.

"Where am I going?" I ask.

"Just get here. Now."

I kiss Andi goodbye, glad Charles didn't call any sooner.

"Tell Walter we'll have a few beers together sometime soon," I tell her. She acts like she believes me.

I have to call Sally Velez and tell her I'm going to be late today and explain why.

"I hope to hell you get a damn story out of this eventually," she says, adding, "And you might want to be careful, for a change."

I promise that I will try.

* * *

THE HOUSE Charles directed me toward necessitates going south off the Zion Crossroads exit, then east, then north again, passing under the interstate. The last turn takes me up one of those Virginia country roads that need to be about ten feet wider. A guy in a pickup almost runs my aged Honda into the trees wheeling around a curve.

And then I see the house. It's brick, two stories, with four columns in front like it's Monticello or something. It sits on a little rise with lots of cleared but fallow land around it. There's a black Denali sitting in the circular driveway in front.

I park in the shade of the behemoth. Whit Charles is standing on the porch overlooking all that land. Gino is leaning against one of the columns, about forty feet away.

Charles has a Budweiser in his hand as he turns toward me. He offers me one when I walk up the steps.

"The old home place," he says, taking a sip and looking around. "Ain't it a beauty?"

It once was impressive enough to have merited a name: Rosewood.

Charles insists that all this will be off the record, just like our last meeting. I dig my heels in a little, because the man seems to be holding a considerably weaker hand than he did last time. He appears to want something from me, so, tit for tat. I tell him that it will be fair game but not for attribution, and that his name won't appear in what I write, if I write it.

He bitches a little but finally agrees. Then he gives me a quick history, something about his great-grandfather, whose name was Rose, buying it with money he won in a poker game, and how now the place is more or less abandoned.

"You own this?" I ask as I light up a Camel, ignoring my host's judgmental frown.

"Yes. After all that unfortunate mess from my guardian days, I was able to hang on to it. Can't do shit with it though."

He takes me inside, explaining as we go how much it would cost to replace the roof, repoint the bricks, put in new windows, replace the flooring, put in central heat, etc., etc., etc. As he talks, a pigeon flies above us, headed back to its nest in one of the dining-room chandeliers.

"Easier to tear it down and start over," he says.

"Why," I ask, "are we here?"

"Because," he says, "they don't know about this place. At least, I hope they don't."

I wait for something other than pigeon shit to descend on me.

"They," it turns out, are the kind of goons who think folks who aren't of the Caucasian persuasion should find some other planet.

"You remember that shit in Charlottesville, right?" Charles asks as he looks up balefully at his bird-nest chandelier.

If he'd been living here in 2017, he wouldn't even ask that question. Who the hell doesn't remember? We'd like to forget, but it's only been a little over two years since the Unite the White rally there that left a young woman and two state cops dead and maybe our state's most liberal city wondering what the fuck happened.

Some of the racist assholes are in jail, and some went back into whatever hole they crawled out of. A few of them, though, apparently decided to retreat and wait for a better, or worse, day. They must have had passports, because they went south.

"Virgin Gorda's pretty laid-back," Charles says. "It's not a bad place to go if you've become *persona non grata* in more, um, civilized climes."

It would be impolite to mention that Whit Charles should know about having to find a new address. His plan is to get back to the British West Indies pretty soon, before family members of some of his former clients know he's here.

Somehow, he says, Stick got involved with these bastards.

"He might have known one of them when he lived in Richmond. At least a couple of them are from Virginia. I know that much."

I'm surprised. Stick Davis was a lot of things when I knew him. He was lazy, a drunk, and world-class inconsiderate. "Racist" was not a box I would have checked. I mean, hell, one of the few people in Richmond who put up with him almost to the end was yours truly, and who did he pick to write his damn memoirs?

"Hell, I really don't think he was ever into all that neo-Nazi shit," Charles says. "He probably just ran into some guys from back home, and they kind of took him in. I'm afraid Stick was what you'd call morally ambiguous."

When Stick found out just how screwed up his new friends were, though, Charles says, he apparently decided to do something about it.

"Stick was in over his head," is the way he describes the situation.

"When he came back to the States, he didn't just take my hundred grand with him. That wouldn't have gotten him killed. It was the plans that got him whacked."

"The plans?"

Charles looks down at Gino, who's just out of earshot.

"The plans to blow up something. Something big. Back here in Virginia. Sometime soon."

I ask him to repeat what he said.

My hearing isn't as good as it once was. It suffered a drastic downhill turn last year when a would-be assassin just missed giving me a bullet lobotomy. Sometimes somebody says something so crazy that I'm sure I misheard.

Charles says it again.

"When? Why?"

I've missed "who," "what," and "where," but Whit can see that he has my attention.

"I don't know all the details," he says. "If I did, maybe we wouldn't be talking here. I'm guessing that they're still pissed about all that mess back in 2017. Maybe wanting to get some payback."

They're pissed? The whole state of Virginia, or at least the great majority of us, would like to kick the shit out of those lunatics for giving the Old Dominion a shiner. You can't have a discussion about skinheads anywhere on the planet without some footage from that godforsaken day. You'd think Charlottesville, aka Berkeley east, was some kind of incubator for Nazis.

If you know all this shit, I ask Charles, why don't you go to the police?

He slaps a yellow jacket away.

"I'm not exactly clean," he says. "I don't mean that I'm involved in any of this crap, but I do have some, ah, unfortunate history up here. I'd just as soon not get involved with the authorities if I can help it."

So, I ask, why the fuck are you here?

"You might not believe it, but I am on the side of the angels on this one. What these guys are planning, I think it will do so much harm that somebody has to do something."

Charles asks me to have a seat.

"I'm going to tell you as much of the story as I know," he says. "I'm going to tell you why I brought Gino up here with me for protection, and why we're meeting out here in God's country where I don't think they can find me."

Sometime after Stick came back home with a bunch of Whit Charles's money, Charles got a note from his former jack-of-all-trades.

The note apologized for what Stick referred to as "the loan" and went on to say that he was working on "something big" involving a group called Purity.

"That was the name of that bunch of thugs he got involved with down there. He said he was afraid of what they were planning, and that he aimed to stop it."

I ask the obvious question: Why the hell didn't Stick go to the cops when he came back up here.

Charles shakes his head.

"I don't know. But he did say something about writing a book about it. I suppose that's where you came in.

"He made one point, though, in the letter. He said he was going to make a big score on this book, he called it an exposé, and also blow the whistle on them in time to stop it from happening. I had the sense that he knew the place and the time, and that he was just biding his time."

He offers me another Bud. I'm a Miller man, but free beer's free beer.

I take the conversation back to why we're out here within eyesight of the middle of nowhere.

"We couldn't talk about this a little closer to Richmond?"

"I had a call this morning. It was from one of those burner phones. Whoever it was had the distinct impression that I knew more than I do. He promised that some rather unpleasant things would happen to me if I didn't cooperate and then get the hell out of Virginia.

"The one I talked to didn't seem to believe me when I told him I didn't know anything. These guys know where I'm staying, and they're serious as a heart attack."

Putting two and two together, it occurs to me that whoever killed Stick Davis didn't get what he was looking for, and that he or they would go to rather extreme measures to obtain it.

"I don't know any more than that," Charles says. "I've made an anonymous call to the FBI, but they didn't seem to take me too seriously. All I know is the name of the group and that something bad is being planned somewhere in Virginia. Not a hell of a lot to go on."

Charles is planning to head back to Virgin Gorda in a couple of days "but I might not be staying there for long. There's other islands, and these lunatics kind of scare me. There was a rumor down there that they took some guy out on a boat, some guy they were afraid was going to rat them out, cut him up, and fed him to the sharks while he was still alive."

The man looks rattled. Considering that he's apparently been something of a criminal himself in recent years, that gets my attention. He does not appear to be the kind of man who scares easily.

He turns to me.

"If I were you," he says, "I'd watch my ass. These guys know who you are."

Yeah, that's occurred to me. If they can read and have access to newspapers or TV, they know who found Stick's body. Maybe they think that I dug up what they weren't able to. Makes sense. I mean, what kind of an asshole has somebody write his memoirs and won't tell him upfront the big secret that's going to make the book a best seller?

Of course, these clowns seem convinced that Whit Charles has been made privy to that information too.

I tell him that what I've written of Stick's life thus far doesn't exactly paint him as a paragon of virtue. Lots of vignettes about drugs and underage girls.

Your name, I say, is mentioned often.

Charles winces.

"Yeah, I figured when I heard what he was doing, I kind of knew there'd be some shit in there that might be uncomfortable for me. Stick was a little too loose of lip, even if he did a lot of good work for me. And I guess those loose lips are what sunk him.

"But that island shit, none of it can be proved, and I sure as hell wouldn't have had him killed over it."

Nevertheless, I put in, I guess you have more than one reason to maybe find another island.

He doesn't deny that.

"Why," I ask when it appears we're winding up, "are you telling me all this?"

He looks at me.

"Because you might be able to get to the bottom of this, or at least get the FBI or somebody involved. You might think I'm the stereotype of a scumbag lawyer, but whatever is going down, I don't want it to happen. There are limits to my depravity. Maybe you can do what I can't."

Charles takes one last swig, crushes the empty beer can, and drops it on the floor.

"Two more days," Charles says. "That's all the time I need to take care of a couple of things, and then I'm out of here."

He looks me in the eye.

"You don't want to buy a house, do you?"

CHAPTER TEN

Wednesday, September 11

After I got back yesterday afternoon, only an hour late for my turn in the night cops barrel, there was an e-mail waiting for me, titled: From Mark.

I assumed that meant Mark Baer, who used to work here before he went rogue and became a flack for a woman who almost became a member of the United States House of Representatives and is lucky not to be in jail at present.

Felicia Delmonico won the election to represent our local congressional district. She also was (a) shown to be ass-deep in an effort to keep some ill-gotten gains hidden and (b) almost killed. The former fact led to the lily-pure members of the House opting not to seat her.

She never got to move to DC, but (a) I understand she's recovering well from being shot by the son of her late husband, Teddy, (b) she's probably going to get away with probation and community service when her fraud case finally comes to trial, (c) she did not, as some suspected, kill said husband, and (d) she has, so far, been able to hang on to the three-million-dollar life-insurance policy Teddy left for her.

Felicia is a survivor—crooked as a blacksnake, but a survivor.

Poor Baer, though, didn't have anything on which to fall back except an otherwise decent résumé besmirched by the fact that he was caught working for the person whose campaign he was supposed to be covering for our newspaper.

I didn't really want to talk to him, but I knew he'd keep bugging me until I did.

He thanked me for getting back with him. As any fool could have foreseen, he was angling to retrace that one-way street he chose and become a journalistic virgin again.

"I really thought she was on the side of the angels," he said. It is hard to believe that anyone who knew Felicia would have been that naive. For the Democrats, she was a means to an end, and when it turned out they didn't need her for a House majority, they set her adrift. Baer was, of course, consigned to a leaky lifeboat with one oar.

"Do you think you could talk to someone there?" he asked. It pained me to hear Baer whine. He could be an asshole and a sneak, but he had always seemed self-sufficient.

I suggested he talk to Sarah. After all, they did "see" each other once upon a time and cut their teeth together here as cub reporters.

A sigh.

"Already did."

I did the thing you do when you don't want to tell the hopeless how hopeless they are. I said he could use me as a reference. I said I'd keep my ears open, knowing full well that I won't hear much that will help Baer.

I asked him if he had been in touch with Ms. Delmonico since the debacle of last year.

"A couple of times. I don't know what she's going to do next, but she said she wasn't looking forward to serving free meals to bums or picking up litter. Oh, and she said to give her a call sometime."

Like that's going to happen, I thought but didn't say. I possibly saved Felicia Delmonico's life last fall, but she isn't calling to thank me. Felicia only calls when she needs something, and it occurred to me that anything I might do to help Felicia probably was going to be a detriment to humanity.

I wished Baer the best and pretty much meant it.

When I mentioned my call to Sarah later that evening, she rolled her eyes.

"Come on," I implored her, giving her my best puppy-dog look. "Don't you think you could help an old buddy, you know, for old times' sake?"

She told me to stuff it.

"Old times here," she said as she closed her office door, "are definitely forgotten."

Sarah, like most journalists high enough up the food chain to be making employment decisions, is in the business of subtracting jobs, not adding them.

* * *

This morning, my first item of business is to drop in on my favorite lawyer. After getting a dose of Whit Charles yesterday, Marcus Green seems almost like an upstanding citizen. To my knowledge, he's never become a client's custodian and then stolen their life savings.

Kate is in the office when I drop by. She asks me when I'm going to send the check for last month's rent.

I do look at my bank statement online occasionally. It's easier than actually writing the amount down each time I send a check, so I know she's bullshitting.

"We've decided to stop paying rent," I tell her. "We're going to be squatters. Saves a lot of money. And if you try to kick us out, I'll start smoking indoors again."

"Aw, crap, Willie," Kate says. "I never could jerk your chain."

That's debatable, but it's nice to be on such jocular terms with at least one of my three exes.

She says Marcus is running late. I ask about Grace, her daughter by her now-deceased second husband.

I suggest that a play date might be nice.

"Willie," she says, "we're past that now."

I quickly explain that I'm talking about having a get-together for Grace, who's in first grade now, and my grandson.

Kate grins.

"Gotcha."

Then she adds, "I don't know, Willie. I don't know if she's into younger men."

He's a charmer, I assert.

"Just like his granddad," Kate says.

Hopefully, I add, not just like him.

Kate doesn't disagree.

Marcus comes in while we're talking. As Kate's third and present husband, he might be concerned about my sitting on the edge of his wife's desk, but he doesn't look worried in the least. Maybe, God forbid, I have aged into the lamentable state of "harmless."

"I tried to call you," he says, "but you didn't answer."

Probably didn't hear it, I say, pointing to my ear.

"Well," Marcus says, "I think we might have shaken something loose on that thing we talked about yesterday."

I was hoping for as much.

Marcus says he put the strong arm on his young client, and it wasn't that hard to get Jerome to confess that there was indeed an iPad among the possessions in Stick Davis's apartment when Jerome was ransacking it, and that he took it.

"I assured him that there wasn't going to be any downside to it, that if anything it might get him a few steps farther away from a future lethal injection. That seemed to get his attention."

The iPad is at his mother's house.

Marcus is happy to have me go with him over to Jerome's mom's place to retrieve the ill-gotten gains.

"Might need backup," he says as we're heading north toward Barton Heights. "The kid says his mother is a bit on the badass side. Hell, being one of Big Boy Sunday's stable, I wouldn't doubt it. Said she might not want to let us in. She's apparently got a problem with people in suits, even if they're of the African American persuasion."

He looks over at me.

"This Jerome," he says, "he's Big Boy's son, isn't he?"

I tell Marcus that this seems obvious to me. Hence the interest on the part of my favorite felon.

"Big Boy's called me twice," he says. "He acts like it'll be my fault if we don't get him out of this. I've explained that the best we can hope for is that he goes down for entering a dead man's house and stealing his stuff. But he'd be tried as a juvenile."

"Well, you cashed the check, right?"

Marcus harrumphs and drives on.

"Let me make a call," I say.

Big Boy Sunday is between meals apparently. I explain the potential problem to him.

"So he stashed away the iPad? Damn, did he think he was going to get out of jail and sell it to somebody? What the fuck's wrong with that boy?"

He agrees that it would be best if he gave Jerome's mom a call to let her know we're coming.

"You're going to get him out of this, though, right, Willie?"

I explain, as politely as I can, that what's on the iPad could go a long way toward ensuring that Jerome doesn't spend much of his remaining life in jail.

"Well," Big Boy says, dragging the word out over three syllables, "I s'pose that's something."

We park in front of the Sheets residence. It's a nice-looking two-story brick house on what, in the light of day, seems like a peaceful-enough street. I've been on this block, though, on nights when the peace had been disturbed big-time.

Ms. Sheets, who goes by Shakira, doesn't really want to let us in, but it's obvious that she's been given her marching orders from Big Boy. Marcus explains that we're here to retrieve something that might help her son's case.

The door is opened, grudgingly.

She's a large woman, the way Big Boy says he likes 'em.

Shakira turns to Marcus, whom she's met only once.

"You're that lawyer," she says, getting very close to his face. "Why you haven't got my Jerome out of jail yet?"

Marcus backs up a step and tries to explain that it isn't that easy getting somebody sprung when there's a dead body involved.

"Jerome ain't killed nobody," she exclaims. "They just setting his ass up."

Then she looks over at me.

"Who the fuck is this?"

Just a reporter looking for the truth, I explain.

"Well," she says, turning her glare on me, "you come to the right place. I can give you all the truth you can eat, Mr. Reporter. And the truth is, I don't need some jumped-up Nee-gro lawyer and whatever the fuck you are coming snooping around here."

Marcus, who can make an unfriendly witness wet his pants in court, seems strangely cowed by Shakira. But he finally gets the point across. Young Jerome took an iPad when he was burglarizing Stick Davis's place, and the cops found no sign of it.

"It could help exonerate him," I offer.

"Exonerate." She repeats it like I've started speaking Chinese. "Yeah, it could exonerate his ass right to prison."

"If I thought that," Marcus says, "would I be here looking for it? I'm his lawyer, Ms. Sheets. I'm the one trying to get him off."

Shakira chews on that for a moment and finally seems to buy it.

What Jerome told Marcus was that the iPad is in his bedroom, hidden between his mattress and box springs.

On the way back to her son's bedroom, I ask Shakira if Jerome is her only child.

She points to a picture hanging on the wall. There's Jerome, all dressed up for church, with two other children, his younger brother and sister.

"He's a good boy," Shakira says. I bite my tongue.

It takes us all of a minute to find the iPad.

"The police never searched here?" I ask.

She snorts.

"The po-po turned the place upside down. Got me out of bed in the middle of the night. Don't guess they looked hard enough."

Marcus thanks Ms. Sheets for her time and tells her that she's done her son a favor by letting us take the iPad.

"You're not gonna give it to the police, are you?"

We assure her that we are not, at least for now, although I'm certain that L.D. Jones and his minions would love to get a look at it.

Tough shit, L.D. Finders keepers. If we dig up something worth reporting to the city's finest, we'll let the chief in on it then. Or maybe I'll let him read it in the paper.

Back in the car, I ask Marcus why he turned into such a pussycat in the face of Shakira Sheets.

He gives me his best baleful stare and tells me he can still kick my ass.

"But you acted like you were afraid she was gonna kick yours."

He drives away from the curb and doesn't answer right away.

Finally, he says, "She reminds me of my momma."

❊ ❊ ❊

We go back to the offices of Green and Ellis. I want to take a look right away, but when we try to access the iPad, it's locked, and we obviously don't know the password.

I have the log-on and password for Stick's computer, the one the cops have. I got a glimpse of it one night when Stick was logging on. He didn't seem to have any problem with my knowing it.

But for whatever reason, Stick has a different log-on and password for the damn iPad, and I don't have that one. It could be in some file on the desktop, but the cops have it, and I doubt if I could induce Peachy to somehow get me access. Plus, I don't want her to know, for her own sake, that I've got something the police would love to get their paws on.

I persuade Marcus to let me take the thing home with me by telling him that I might have a couple of ideas of what the password might be.

He shrugs.

"Might as well. I don't have a clue. But we need to get it to the cops, soon."

I go back by the Prestwould long enough to stash it. I have an idea that might or might not be full of shit. I'll play around with that iPad tomorrow and see if I'm right.

❊ ❊ ❊

I WASTE the rest of the morning or early afternoon waiting for the bandits at my favorite garage to get through inspecting the Honda. Virginia, either to make the highways safer or to line the pockets of mechanics, dictates that we have to get our vehicles inspected once a year.

With the Honda, it's always something. Hell, the damn thing has almost two hundred thousand miles on it.

This time, it's the brakes.

"How much," I ask the young guy who gives me the bad news like a doctor telling you you've got Stage 4 cancer, "would you take to just put the damn sticker on and look the other way?"

He seems offended.

Two hours later and a few hundred dollars lighter, the Accord and I make our escape.

I stop at a burger joint on the way in and get to the paper not long after I was supposed to be there.

When I report for duty, I see Wheelie, Sarah, and Benson Stine, our present publisher, in what appears to be serious conversation in Wheelie's office. I know it's serious because Wheelie is doing that thing he does when he's presented with a plate-load of crap. He grips the arms of his chair tight, as if to prevent himself from flying over the desk and strangling someone. So far, Wheelie has held tight.

The office, as with the rest of the editors' digs, is enclosed by glass, so the whole newsroom can see that something's happening here, but since none of us are lip-readers, what it is ain't exactly clear.

"Probably trying to decide whether to give us 5 percent or 10 percent raises next year," Sally Velez says. No one even bothers to laugh.

When their little confab breaks up, I wait half an hour and then mosey over to Sarah's small office.

"Don't even ask me, Willie," she says when she sees me standing in the door.

* * *

It's a quiet afternoon and evening, until it isn't.

About eight, I get a call. It's my accountant, who normally only calls in April to give me bad news.

He lives in a posh neighborhood out off Three Chop Road, close to the University of Richmond. He seems excited to be giving me a hot news tip. Hell, the guy probably needs a little excitement.

"There's something going on out here, Willie," he says. "All hell's breaking loose."

I ask him to be more specific.

He says that about half the cop cars and ambulances in the city seem to have converged on a house in the next block.

"Somebody said they found a couple of dead bodies," he adds.

That gets my attention.

He's outside, and I can hear the cacophony of sirens in the background.

He's in a neighborhood where nobody dies. They just move to Westminster Canterbury. After paying about 10K a month for "assisted living" bed and board, they eventually die there if they don't run out of money first.

"This can't be good for real-estate values," I observe.

"Damn, Willie," my accountant says, "that's cold."

I'm on my way in five minutes. I can't tell a damn bit of difference in the brakes.

There are six police and other emergency vehicles on the tight little street, which I'm sure doesn't see a lot of action unless UR has a home football or basketball game. Neighbors are standing in their yards.

I park as close as I can. Call it intuition, but the hairs on my arms are standing up.

And then I see the Black Denali parked in the driveway.

The house is a big-ass brick Tudor monstrosity, probably the property of some old ambulance-chasing buddy of Whit Charles.

No one else from the news media is here yet, but I know they'll be hot on my heels. The TV folk will have something on the eleven o'clock news that their viewers don't already know about for a change.

Among the uniforms standing in the chill and watching the red, blue, and yellow blinking lights reflect off the house's windows is my old buddy Gillespie.

He greets me warmly.

"What the fuck," he asks, "are you doing here?"

I don't bother with the obvious answer.

"Two bodies?" I ask.

He looks around like he thinks L.D. Jones might be watching. He nods.

Gillespie hasn't been in the house. He says the cops got a call a couple of hours ago, from a neighbor who thought he heard gunshots from inside.

I walk across the well-tended lawn. Just as I'm getting close to the front door, it opens. Four EMTs come out carrying a covered stretcher. And then four more come out with a second one. They don't seem to be in a hurry.

Then L.D. comes through the door. I catch up with the chief as he hits the brick walkway.

He greets me much as Gillespie did earlier.

"Do you know who they are?" I ask him.

He tells me it's none of my fucking business who they are, and to stop interfering with police business.

"Would you like me to tell you?" I ask.

CHAPTER ELEVEN

Thursday, September 12

I was pretty sure whom I was going to find under those sheets last night. And there they were.

Whit Charles looked reasonably intact, although I could see that one of his hands was missing all its fingers. Gino, who didn't turn out to be much of a bodyguard after all, took a couple to the face. He was still barely recognizable, although open casket is out of the question.

When I told the chief who they were, he was several levels beyond interested.

"So this guy, the one on the right, was Randolph Davis's employer down there in the islands? And how the fuck did you know that?"

L.D. informed me that I was again waist deep in the big muddy when it comes to Stick's murder.

I had no choice but to tell the chief how I came to know Charles. I told him about the concerns the guy had about his safety.

"And you've never been here to this house before? And yet you knew who was under those sheets, before we even showed you the bodies."

L.D. was not appeased when I told him I knew generally where Charles was staying, that I knew he drove a black

Denali, and that he seemed sure some very bad men were trying to get something they thought he had. I told him I had a hunch as soon as I heard about the two bodies.

The chief, not a great believer in hunches, said I needed to start talking "right damn now." I asked him if I could send in a story to the paper first. He told me I'd be lucky if my next story wasn't sent from the city jail.

He and a couple of his detectives directed me into the house. The place was a wreck. Whoever let Charles house-sit definitely is going to have to do some major remodeling.

"Like they were looking for something," the chief says. He adds that neither victim seemed to have been robbed.

That, I explained to L.D., is what I've been trying to tell you. Somebody thought Charles had something they wanted.

By this time, the four of us were sitting in the living room, them on the couch and me on an ottoman facing them.

"If I knew what," I told them, "I'd be a lot happier."

I remind the chief about the guys Mrs. Woolfolk saw go into Stick's place the day before I found his body, who left with paper bags full of something. I tell him again about Stick's notebooks that weren't there later when I was allowed to look.

"Why didn't she tell us about it?"

"Again, dammit, because nobody asked her."

The chief looked like he wanted to hit somebody.

Taking it a step further, I said that a friend of Stick's told me that he had an iPad where he seemed to keep something he didn't want on his desktop computer.

"Did we find an iPad?" he asked one of the detectives, who shook his head.

He turned his bloodshot eyes to me.

"So, you knew there were some missing notebooks, and that a couple of unknown males were in the victim's home after he was killed, and now there's this missing iPad."

"I wasn't sure what all this meant. I'm still not."

"Bullshit. You just wanted to get a damn story out of it."

Yeah, I could have told the chief that I was in possession of that iPad, which the cops would have found themselves if they'd done a better job of searching Jerome's mom's house. But I kind of promised Ms. Sheets. Mainly, though, I wanted to get the first crack at whatever was so damned important.

It occurred to me that if Whit Charles had been aware of that iPad, he might have had something he could have traded for his life.

The chief and his minions grilled me for an hour and a half, long enough to keep me from getting any of the details of the double homi into tomorrow's paper. All I could do was post it on our website, much to the irritation of Sally Velez, whose earlier calls L.D. did not allow me to answer.

When they were finally convinced that I almost certainly could not have killed Charles and Gino, the chief said I could go, but not to leave town.

On the way out, he pulled me aside.

"If you're holding out on me," he said, "you better watch your ass. This isn't just your usual junior detective shit. These guys, whoever they are, they don't fuck around. If you've got something they want, you are not safe."

He told me then details I was not allowed to print. Gino had been dispatched pretty quickly, it seemed, but Whit Charles apparently was bound and gagged and more or less tortured to death.

"Believe me," L.D. said, "if the guy had what they were after, he would have given it to them. They had started on the other hand, and maybe he bled to death or just had a heart attack. I don't know what finally killed him, but he was probably glad to go, from what we saw."

The chief had my attention. It occurred to me that Whit Charles might have told his killers about the nosy-ass reporter who also had access to Stick Davis's apartment.

One shot at the iPad, I promised myself, and then I'll turn it over to the cops.

* * *

And so, here I am. I have the tablet in front of me, taunting me.

Cindy's already at work. I gave her the shorthand version of my busy night. I didn't even tell her that I had the iPad, but I did call Marcus this morning.

"You need to give that thing to the cops right damn now," he said. "If you don't, I'm going to give them a call."

I tell him to give me a couple of hours. I don't think Marcus is all that concerned about my well-being, but he's very fond of his own health and happiness.

I try several log-ons and passwords, variations of the ones Stick Davis used on his home computer, but nothing works. I try his first name, his middle name, his birth date, even Terri McAllister's first and last names.

Then I give my hunch from the day before a shot. Apple pie with ice cream and a longshot horse.

I try à la mode as a log-in and bumpass as a password, then drop the French shit and just spell it alamode, and then I try Bumpass with a capital B, and voilà. Open sesame.

After fiddling around for a few minutes, I try the "Notes" icon. The only note inside the icon is slugged "Jordan."

Jordan, as in Jordan's Branch. The creek that once ran by Westwood, where Stick was living, and is now buried beneath the median strip on Willow Lawn Drive.

Stick has rather cryptic instructions about what to do "should anything happen to me." So cryptic, in fact, that I don't really know what the fuck he's talking about at first.

"Look for Jordan's Branch," he tells me from the Great Beyond. "East of Dunbar. Look for two bricks. That's the spot. Dig." And that's all the note says.

Since Jordan's Branch is buried beneath a busy street at present, this doesn't help me much.

I know I've seen that damn creek somewhere else in Richmond. So I get out my area map and start looking. It first appears above ground some blocks away from Westwood, and it eventually, after a million twists and turns, runs into the Chickahominy River north of the city. I remember now crossing it on Staples Mill Road. But that's probably a mile from Stick's last address.

Sitting there and yearning for a Camel, I wonder how long those guys tortured old Stick before they finally put him out of his misery. I'm guessing they looked on his home computer and didn't find anything there, and then they or somebody else had to come back later for the notebooks. We don't seem to be dealing with geniuses. In the meantime, in the course of one of young Mr. Sheets's more unfortunate juvenile criminal moves, he absconded with the iPad. He probably left the computer because it was too unwieldy to haul off.

But then I go back and look at the map again. And then I see it. On the east side of Westwood, the side I never saw in my visits to Stick's house, there it is. Dunbar. It runs parallel to Willow Lawn Drive, with a row of houses between the two streets.

East of Dunbar.

Well, who doesn't love a scavenger hunt? Stick Davis must be laughing his ass off, thinking of me going down to Abe Custalow's little office in the Prestwould basement and asking him if he has a shovel.

"What for?"

I convince him that it is in his best interest if he doesn't know.

"Do you want me to come with you?" he asks, not even knowing where I'm going. Abe has been my salvation more than once when I've rushed in where angels or sane people fear to tread.

I tell him that I appreciate it, and I might be calling on his ass soon, but I feel pretty safe right now.

"This is about Stick Davis, isn't it?"

I nod as he hands me the shovel. I leave before he can ask me anything else or run after me.

OK, I'm thinking. Just as soon as I get my hands on whatever Stick's buried in the median of Willow Lawn Drive, I'll put everything in the somewhat capable hands of Richmond's finest.

* * *

I drive out Patterson Avenue, turn right, and park near where Dunbar and Willow Lawn converge before the latter pulls away from it, following the path of the now-buried Jordan's Branch.

Looking at the map, I see that the place Stick mentioned could be anywhere in the next hundred yards or so.

I get out of the car, put out my cigarette, take the shovel out of the trunk, and start walking up the median strip, ignoring curious stares from passersby on Willow Lawn.

The bricks are maybe fifty yards up. I almost miss them at first. They are mostly buried in the grass, side by side. They are low enough that city crews, should they ever mow out here, wouldn't strike them.

I've dug a foot or so when the shovel strikes something hard. I get down on my hands and knees and dig out a metal box, maybe eight inches square, four inches deep.

Inside it, double-wrapped in plastic bags, is a DVD.

By now, it's close to noon. I drive back to the Prestwould and go up to our apartment. The Blu-ray player Cindy insisted we had to have has a DVD slot.

I pop the disc in.

On the video, there are two men seated at a table, with a cloth hung behind them. In front of the cloth are a Nazi flag and our Dixie favorite, the Confederate battle flag.

The men are both literal skinheads, with necks about the same circumference as their heads. Both are wearing masks that cover the bottom half of their faces. This does not keep me from seeing the tattoo across one of their foreheads. It reads "Purity."

One of them speaks:

"If you are watching this," he says, "you know what we have done. The righteous mayhem we have unleashed is just a hint of what is to come. We are myriad, and we will emerge victorious over the mongrels and their lackeys. Today Virginia, tomorrow the world. We are Purity."

They stand and give a Nazi salute. The video ends.

I am silent. While I was watching, Custalow came into the apartment for his lunch break. I don't hear him until he says, "Shit," making me jump about a foot. "What the hell is that?"

Something, I tell him, that needs to be in the hands of somebody smarter and better-armed than a night cops reporter.

* * *

I CALL Marcus to tell him, in general terms, what I found, and then I head down to police headquarters.

L.D. is out to lunch when I get there. Somehow I put enough fear into his snot-nosed aide to get him to contact the chief and put me on with him.

"I have something that's scaring the shit out of me," I tell him. "You have to see this."

I have L.D.'s attention, apparently. He's back in ten minutes with a speck of mustard on his chin.

"This had better be good," he warns.

We watch the skinheads' performance together.

"And you've had this how long?" the chief asks.

Just since this morning, I answer. I tell him where it was buried, not mentioning that I've had the iPad with the necessary directions since yesterday.

L.D. is not a complete idiot. He presses me on how exactly I came to know where to dig. I have to tell him about the iPad.

"Look," I say, only lying a little, "the Sheets kid's mother found it in his room, and she called Marcus Green, and he and I went and got it. I just wanted to see for myself what it was about before I turned it over to you. And I found the note that told me where to dig."

I remind him of all the things linking the late Whit Charles to Stick and to whoever made that video.

"Suppressing evidence," the chief mutters. I can tell, though, that the DVD has his attention, and that maybe tossing me in jail for withholding the iPad for a day or so isn't at the top of his list. He isn't even interested, for now, in why an accused murderer's mom would want anyone to know about something else the kid had stolen.

Like me, his attention is on the DVD.

"There's no date or anything on it? Nothing to tell us when they're talking about?"

I shake my head.

"What you see is all I've got."

I know L.D. likes to go it alone, that he hates to call in outside help. It's something we have in common. When he says, "We need to take this on up the ladder," he's showing me he knows he's in over his head.

By "outside help," I'm sure he doesn't mean the mayor. In a few minutes, he's contacted the state police and the FBI.

I tell the chief that I have to get to work. It's almost two o'clock.

"As soon as we get everybody together," he says, "your ass is back here, understand? You might have stuck your nose a little too close to the hornet's nest this time."

I remind him that being made a suspect in a murder case kind of gave me the right to stick my nose in. I also tell him that I'm going to write about what I've seen and heard so far.

"If you write one word of this," he says, sticking his finger in my face, "I will have you arrested."

I remind him that he wouldn't have shit if it weren't for me.

"Yeah," he says, "and if you'd have taken that damn iPad straight to us, we might have had a day's head start on figuring out what these crackers are planning, and when."

It would feel good to tell L.D. that, if I had given the iPad to his bonehead department directly, it probably would still be moldering in the evidence room.

We finally reach an accommodation.

I will write about the police gaining possession of a valuable piece of evidence in the death of Randolph Giles "Stick" Davis, and that there are indications that his death and the killings of lawyer and former Virginia resident Whitney Charles and one Gino Morelli, address unknown, could be tied to Davis's murder.

No mention of an iPad, or any of the particulars that left a certain DVD in the hands of Richmond's finest. I'll even have a quote from the chief:

"We have been diligently searching for answers in this case. The evidence we have now goes a long way toward solving these crimes and achieving justice."

The story also will note that one Jerome Sheets, incarcerated in regard to the Davis murder, is no longer considered a prime suspect, although he is still, of course, on the hook for breaking and entering.

That should make Marcus Green, Shakira Sheets, and Big Boy Sunday at least moderately happy.

"Am I off the hook too?" I ask the chief.

He says he'll tell me when I'm off the hook.

* * *

I head back to the paper.

As is often the case these days, there is news. Unsurprisingly it is not good.

"They've sold the building," Sally Velez informs me even before I can go for my first cup of newsroom coffee.

It seems that the Grimm Group, in a frantic attempt to drain every last ounce of blood out of our anemic operation, has indeed sold our premises out from under us. Well, not exactly. The new owners, a bunch of local real-estate development sharpies, are willing to let us rent space in what is now their digs.

Our old masters lost this place through their incredible farsightedness. They borrowed big-time to buy some damn TV stations just before the goddamn market collapsed and the whole world realized that advertising in and reading newspapers was so twentieth century.

That was light years and two owners ago.

These days, we can put the whole shebang—the suits, advertising, promotions, the newsroom, everything—on one floor of this white elephant.

And that's what they're going to do.

Even Stine, our revered publisher, will have to move into what, for him, will seem like paupers' digs and hobnob with the hoi polloi. That should be good.

I ask Sarah about Luther Gates. She says he's still at large, and that she's looking forward to meeting him "so I can kneecap his ass."

I counsel her to be careful what she wishes for.

"We have bigger things to talk about," I tell her and ask her to get Wheelie to join us.

When we all gather in Wheelie's office, I tell them what I can write and what I know. Full disclosure for a change.

"So somebody's planning to wreak havoc on something in Virginia, and we can't tell anybody about it?" Wheelie says.

I explain that that's what I promised. And when they catch these bozos, I assure them, we'll have the whole story.

"If they catch them in time," Sarah says.

There is really no other way to go. Our readers will know that new evidence is pointing to someone other than a night cops reporter or a kid thief killing Stick Davis. They will know that the two murders that made our website after midnight might be connected to Mr. Davis.

They won't know that the same people might be planning to blow a great big hole somewhere in their home state.

I am put in the tenuous position of putting my safety and that of my fellow Virginians in the hands of the authorities. And, what the fuck, if we told the readers that something, somewhere in the state was going to go boom sometime, what would that do except cause people to crap themselves and hide under the bed?

* * *

I have just finished tying everything together for tomorrow's readers: the two deaths last night plus the "new evidence" tying those to Stick's murder, when I get a call.

I don't recognize the voice.

"You're sticking your nose into something that doesn't concern you," it says.

I play dumb, not that big a stretch.

"Who are you? What are you talking about?"

All the voice says is "Stick Davis."

I wait.

And then he adds the kicker.

"We know where you live, nigger. You and your wife and that half-breed Indian. What's his name? Oh, yeah. Custalow."

Passing as I usually do for white, I'm taken aback by both the slur and the fact that evil is a lot closer to my ass than I realized. What did Whit Charles tell them as they were lopping off his fingers? But Charles didn't know about the DVD. Not possible. He just knew there were bad guys out there planning some bad shit.

"Who are you?" I ask.

"Never mind who we are, asshole," he says. "But you've got something we want, and you'll give it back if you know what's good for you."

At this point, a wiser soul would plead ignorance.

But this guy, whoever he is, is pissing me off.

"You're right. I do have something of yours."

"Oh, yeah," he says. "Tell me about it."

I'm making it up as I go along.

"It's going to cost you to get it back," I tell him. "You and your pal look really good on camera."

He's silent for a minute. I'm thinking the guy knows there's a DVD out there with his ugly mug on it, one that maybe would tip off the cops and spoil these monsters' fun. I'm counting on the fact that he's figuring I'm a money-grubbing bastard who'd sell anything for the right price, rather than pass it on to the cops. People have such a low opinion of professional journalists.

"How much?"

"I'm thinking a quarter of a million."

"You fuckin' jungle bunny," he says.

"Well," I reply, "I could just pass it on to the police."

He's quiet for a bit. Then it sounds like he's talking to somebody else in the background.

"Yeah," he says at last, "we can do that. Tomorrow. I'll call you with a time and place. Two hours."

What, I ask myself as I hang up, have I done?

CHAPTER TWELVE

The guy called about seven thirty, which leaves me with a lot to do in a little time.

I call Cindy and tell her she needs to pack her bags and move in with her sister for a couple of days.

"Was it something I did?" she asks.

I explain, making it sound as unthreatening as possible.

"I'm just worried, you know. Nothing serious, but they do know where we live."

"Nothing serious? What the fuck, Willie? If it wasn't serious, you wouldn't be sending me to my damn sister's house. What the hell have you gotten us into?"

I explain that I am trying, for once, to do something good.

"And Custalow needs to go over and stay at Stella Stellar's for a couple of days."

"She's on the road," Cindy says.

"He has the key to her place."

I tell her to let me speak to Abe, who's probably getting ready to watch Thursday Night Football.

"Do you need help?" he asks when I tell him what's going on.

I explain that my next call is to L.D. Jones, who should have rounded up a posse of state and federal cops by now.

He passes the phone back to Cindy.

"If you get your ass killed," she says, "I'll never speak to you again."

* * *

THE CHIEF calls me as I'm about to phone him.

"You need to get down here," he says. "Right now."

You don't know, I explain to him, how much I need to get down there.

I'm expecting to hear from my anonymous caller sometime soon. I explain this to L.D.

"You did what?" he shouts. "Are you out of your fuckin' mind? You're way above your grade this time, Willie."

Then he asks me for the number of the guy who called my cell. I'm sure it will turn out to be a burner phone.

"But this guy, from Purity or whatever the fuck, he's going to call you back?"

I explain that he could call at any time, probably on another burner phone, and that this is one call I definitely need to take.

"Well, hell. Get your ass over here, and if he calls you on the way, you can take it in the car."

The chief tells me what any fool would already have figured out. We don't know what, when, or where, and the clock is ticking.

"Why the fuck do you think I'm doing this?" I ask. "You think I'm doing this for my health?"

I tell Sarah, who's the night adult supervision, what's going on, and how Chuck Apple or somebody else will have to deal with whatever carnage Richmonders visit upon each other for the rest of the evening.

"You're an idiot," Sarah says as I'm leaving. She walks me to the elevator, turns to see that no one else in our near-empty newsroom is looking, and gives me a quick kiss on the lips. "Be careful," she says.

I tell her I've never been so pleasantly sexually harassed. She gives me the finger as the door closes.

* * *

My cell buzzes on the car seat beside me as I'm looking for a parking space next to police headquarters. I flout the law by answering while circling the block, then pull into a no-parking space.

"Here's the time and place," the same voice from before says. "Make sure you get it right, and you better make damn sure you're alone."

He reminds me again that he knows where I live.

"Might just have to blow up the whole damn building if you fuck with us," he says, throwing in a racial pejorative for free.

I can't imagine the Prestwould imploding onto Franklin Street. Wouldn't McGrumpy be pissed?

The address he gives me is not far from the house where Stick was murdered. Actually it's only a stone's throw from the place above the subterranean Jordan's Branch where I found those two bricks and the DVD. The house is on a part of West Franklin Street far from my downtown digs. The street where I live gets cut off by the Downtown Expressway and then picks up again headed farther west.

The voice tells me to be there at nine P.M. tomorrow.

"Got that?"

I reply that I do.

"Damn well better," he says and hangs up.

Inside police headquarters, I'm directed to a big-ass conference room where the cream of law enforcement from our area code seems to have gathered. I'm introduced to none of them, but they already know who I am, compliments of L.D. Actually "insults of L.D." probably is more accurate. I assume the ones in suits are feds of various sorts. The state police contingent is in uniform, as are L.D. and several of his minions.

When I tell them the Purity guy gave me a time and a place to meet, they seem put out that I didn't somehow keep the guy on the phone long enough for them to figure out where he was calling from.

"You really ought to leave this to the professionals," one of the suits advises. I advise him to smooch my nether parts.

The chief explains to the now-offended suit that I'm an asshole, but that we all need to work together.

"And, like it or not, this idiot is all we've got."

"So," one of the state cops says, "are we going to let him go out there?"

They speak among themselves for a bit, talking around me as if I were a piece of inconvenient office furniture.

"What if they just kill him and take the DVD?" one of the detectives asks. He doesn't seem saddened by that scenario.

"Obviously he won't have it with him," another fed says. "That would be crazy."

"They probably won't have the money either," a third one throws in.

So, I ask, interrupting this discussion of my future, what should I do?

Thinking about the mess these fuckers made of Whit Charles and Gino, to say nothing of Stick Davis, I opine that I am somewhat concerned about my personal safety.

"Of course," L.D. says, "we'll be tracking you."

"How do they know that you aren't just setting them up?" one of his detectives asks me.

"Beats me. But do you have any better ideas?"

They don't. They're already pretty sure that the phones the bad guys used are lying in a ditch somewhere by now, and the only other people Purity has contacted about getting their purloined property back are currently dead.

Like it or not, I'm it.

What the assembled brain trust agrees on is that these guys probably see me as a money-grubbing dirtbag trying to make a buck, rather than a civic-minded citizen.

"And Willie's had kind of a checkered past," the chief helpfully throws in.

I point out that three divorces and a fondness for booze and Camels don't exactly make me Public Enemy Number One.

"Yeah, yeah," L.D. says, waving away my indignation. "We might know that, but an outsider, checking up on you, might see you as somebody that could be compromised. And these guys have obviously checked up on you."

One of the feds tells me things I already know about Purity and some that I don't.

"They were there in Charlottesville," he says. "They managed to get away without getting arrested, somehow, although some of them would have been if they hadn't gone underground. They're basically anarchists. They want the whole country to start killing one another, turn the blacks, the whites, the Jews, the Muslims, everybody against each other. Helter-Skelter shit. And then they think they'll take over."

They're suspected in an attack on a black church down in North Carolina and in a bombing incident at the home of an African American mayor up in Ohio.

"Probably other stuff too," he says. "But we hadn't heard from them in a while. We kind of hoped they'd disbanded."

"Or gone to hell," one of his fed buddies mutters.

L.D. has filled them in on what I learned from Charles.

"It makes sense," the state cop says. "They've been down there in the islands planning this shit all along. They probably want payback for Charlottesville. Like we're not the ones who ought to be paying them back. Bastards."

Two state police officers died trying to control that shit storm in Charlottesville when their helicopter crashed. It kind of got lost in all the furor about the poor woman who was killed by some neo-Nazi's kamikaze car, but the state cops sure as shit haven't forgotten it.

So they come up with a plan. They assure me that they will have their eyes and ears on me the whole time, from a few blocks away. We agree to meet again at police headquarters tomorrow morning to firm things up.

What could possibly go wrong?

⁂ ⁂ ⁂

I LET Sally Velez and Sarah know that I won't be in for the rest of the evening.

L.D. suggests that I go somewhere other than home tonight. I assure him I will do so and that the other residents of my rented apartment are vacating the premises.

"So where are you going?"

I haven't thought much about that. I was too concerned with getting Cindy and Abe to safety.

It occurs to me that I know at least one person who probably won't be all tucked in before the eleven o'clock news is over.

R.P. McGonnigal, who changes boyfriends like most people change shirts, is hooked up with his latest in

Rocketts Landing, a development along the river east of town, maybe a ten-minute drive from here. He's always been an insomniac. When we were kids in Oregon Hill, he claimed he slept about three hours a day. He snoozes more than that now. He's more of a late-to-bed, late-to-rise type, and I guess and hope his latest amour dances to the same circadian rhythm.

"Sure," R.P. says without hesitation when I call and explain that I need a place to sleep tonight, without getting into the messy details. "We were just getting ready to watch a movie. You can sleep on the couch. I'm making popcorn."

I ask him if popcorn goes well with bourbon. He says that apparently it does.

I keep an eye on the rearview mirror on the way out of town. If these assholes know enough about me to know that I might have the DVD they covet, they could be smart enough to be following me.

Nothing suspicious shows up, though, as I work my way down East Main past Millie's and Poe's Pub.

R.P. has a condo that, although it's within smelling distance of the river, has no view of it. He introduces me to Brooklyn, who I am told is called that "because that's where I'm from" in an accent that verifies the statement.

I tell my old friend and his buddy most of the rest of the story about why I'm here, not mentioning the meeting that's set for tomorrow night. The cops, I explain, just think it would be good if I didn't go back to the Prestwould until they busted these guys.

"Oh, I figured Cindy had kicked your ass out," he says, and proceeds to give Brooklyn what I consider to be an overly embellished account of my matrimonial history.

"Jeez," Brooklyn says, "I've always said they shouldn't let you people marry."

R.P. wonders, as any sane person would, whether I'm tracking danger into their cozy abode. I assure them that I wasn't followed, and that this is a one-night stand.

"Well," he says, "I guess if they break the door down, maybe they'll just shoot you there on the couch and leave us alone."

"Those fuckers don't like gays, either, do they?" Brooklyn asks.

Probably not, I concur.

* * *

I CALL Cindy from their bedroom while they're watching a movie where, it seems, nothing is going to blow up.

She says she's safe and sound at her sister's, and that Abe presumably is hunkering down at Stella Stellar's.

"Why do you get into messes like this?" she asks.

I explain that this one was forced upon me when I found Stick Davis's body and became, for a time, Suspect Number One in his murder. Trying to clear myself seemed like a good idea.

"But if you didn't hang out with people like that, you wouldn't be all the time gettin' your ass in a sling," she says. "Why can't you associate with nicer people?"

"I associate with you."

"Well," she says, "I'm not feeling so nice right now."

She lowers her voice and tells me that her sister and brother-in-law apparently aren't getting along that well.

"They got in a big argument right in front of me. I appreciate them keeping me, but I'm as uneasy as a whore in church. I miss my own bed. I miss you in it."

On top of that, she says, her worthless son, the Chipster, e-mailed her today trying once again to get her to throw some of her money down the rathole he calls his latest effort to become a restaurateur.

I tell Cindy that we're hoping to wrap this whole mess up tomorrow night. I don't tell her that wrapping it up entails me going into a strange house full of racist neo-Nazis who obviously would kill for an object they only think I have.

No point in spoiling her beauty sleep.

As for my own forty winks, I get maybe twenty of them. The sofa bed works better as the former than the latter. And R.J. and Brooklyn get bored with the movie halfway through but are wired enough afterward to expend the rest of their energy in their king-sized bed, making noises I won't be able to un-hear for some time.

In addition, my mind keeps coming back to my present situation. No number of leaping sheep can prevent me from walking through various scenarios in my mind and posing unanswerable questions.

What if these bastards shoot my ass as soon as I get there, cops be damned?

What if the cops get a little careless and let the bad guys carry me off to parts unknown?

What if some trigger-happy flatfoot or G-man just goes into "let God sort 'em out" mode and starts shooting indiscriminately?

Sometimes an active imagination can be a curse.

CHAPTER THIRTEEN

Friday, September 13

Friday the thirteenth probably is not the best day to test your luck. Sometimes, though, you just work with the hand you're dealt and pray for an inside straight.

After a restful four hours of sleep, I accept R.J.'s offer of a bagel and a cup of coffee, take a shower, and hit the road. He says the sofa bed is mine if I want it for another night or three. I tell him that I hope that won't be necessary.

I am painfully aware that I'm going to need to run by the Prestwould for at least ten minutes to change underwear and pack a few essentials in case this is not just a one-night hiatus.

Feldman, aka McGrumpy, is in the lobby as usual when I drop by about nine thirty.

"Killed anybody lately?" my favorite pain in the ass asks.

"Not this morning, but the day's still young. I'm thinking seriously about it," I inform him.

I do tell Marcia the manager about the bad guys who are dying to meet me, talking low enough that the half-deaf Feldman can't hear. I assure her that I'm staying away from the old home place until things calm down. I cross my fingers and tell her there's no need for anybody at the Prestwould to worry.

She does not look worried exactly, but she's not exuding serenity either.

"If somebody comes here looking for me," I tell her, "tell them I've moved out for a few days."

I look over at the chair where McGrumpy is trying to get a fellow resident to sign a petition demanding that we throw out the condo board of directors and cut the monthly fee.

"If they want to take a hostage," I tell Marcia, "give them Feldman.

"Just kidding," I add.

Marcia whispers that the hostage thing sounds like a good idea.

She giggles.

"Except after a day or so, they'd probably make us take him back."

* * *

I call Cindy on the way to huddle with L.D. and the rest of the law-enforcement brain trust and tell her where I slept last night.

"Well, if you need to hide out again, there's a queen bed over here that's half empty."

If there's a god, I tell her, we'll both be sleeping back at the Prestwould tonight.

There's coffee and, of course, donuts at police headquarters. Most of last night's assemblage and a few extras are here. Some of the cops are having to eat standing up. I'm supposed to be tight-lipped about this caper, but it seems like every flatfoot in the city is in on it. I even see Gillespie over in the corner with Krispy Kreme dust on his fat face.

The feds have checked out the place we're supposed to meet off Willow Lawn. The house belongs to somebody who's turned it into an Airbnb rental.

"The guy says it's rented to the same group for the next five days," one of them says. "When I told him they might be fugitives, he wanted us to go over and help him kick them out right then. I convinced him that he'd be doing us all a big favor if he let it slide and kept his mouth shut for a couple of days."

Hard to believe an up-and-up operation like Airbnb could be involved in something like this. One of my neighbors at the Prestwould tried to make some money renting by the day. He had college kids throwing parties in his unit until the board figured out what he was doing.

The rental is in the name of some woman who, the fed says, is a relative of one of the Purifiers.

Among them, the feds, state cops, and locals, they do have a plan, one that I'm assured will expose me to minimal risk. I make it clear that I'd prefer no risk at all. The head fed says they'll do the best they can.

The way it's supposed to play out, I'm to show up at the front door of the place on far West Franklin Street at nine tonight, as promised.

I won't have the DVD with me. I'm supposed to tell them that I've gotten nervous and have put it away at another location, where I have a couple of friends waiting, armed to the teeth, to make sure the deal goes as planned.

The brain trust has decided I won't be wearing a wire. If the Purity assholes agree to give me the quarter-million I've asked for, I'm to lead them to a house a couple of blocks away that the feds have commandeered. The big brains think it would be better for me to lead them there rather than storming the Airbnb.

"And then we'll have them and we will see if we can persuade them to tell us the when and where."

He adds, "It's not likely they'll have the quarter-million anyhow."

"So they would just kill me and take the DVD."

"Yes," the guy says, "but that's what we're here for. To protect you."

The phrase, "I'm from the government and I'm here to help" pops into my head.

Any persuasion visited on these pieces of crap is fine with me. I do want to know, though, what happens if things don't go quite as planned. Like what if they just decide to shoot my ass out of frustration if I don't produce the DVD, which I won't have, or they take me hostage and promise to starting chopping off fingers until I see things their way. Wouldn't take long. I remind the cops about what these same fine citizens did to Whit Charles.

"We will be monitoring everything from that house two blocks away," I am told. "If anything looks like it's going wrong, use this."

One of the feds hands me a cell phone. It looks like mine, and he says they can transfer everything off my phone to this one, including the number. But there is one small difference.

"Just push the home button twice. You can do that even if it's still in your pocket. It's set up to send us an emergency signal, and we'll be there in thirty seconds."

Here's hoping, I tell them.

Some tech geek does the transferring, and I'm good to go. Well, I needed a new phone anyhow. Who said I wouldn't get something out of this?

* * *

I'M NOT supposed to talk to anyone about this, but the hell with that. I want Wheelie and Sarah to know so that if this turns out to be a major clusterfuck, with me as the fuckee, somebody will get a heapin' helping of retribution.

Before I report to the newsroom, though, I have time to check in with Peggy. I don't want my old mom to worry, but maybe it'd be good if she had some idea why I've been a little busy lately.

She and Awesome Dude are sitting in the living room, watching a TV show in which a nine-hundred-pound man is trying to save himself, presumably by getting down to a more svelte six hundred or so.

"How in the world do people get like that?" Awesome inquires.

"Girl Scout cookies?" I ask, looking at the mostly devoured sleeve lying on the coffee table in front of Awesome and Peggy.

"I was hungry," my mom says.

Considering that the two of them pretty much have terminal munchies, it is hard to understand how they, too, don't weigh nine hundred pounds.

I explain my present situation, making it sound more like a caper than something that could get my ass killed.

"So that's some of the same bastards that was in Charlottesville?" Peggy asks. "I hope they shoot 'em."

My mom, who bore a son by an African American, is inclined to be prejudiced against bigots.

"So you're in the clear now about killing that Stick fella?" Peggy asks.

Yes, I assure her, there is that to be happy about.

I also assure her that I will be well-protected. I don't go into the details of tonight's little get-together, but I'm pretty sure neither Peggy nor Awesome is fully engaged in our conversation and might lose memory of it in a marijuana fog by the time I'm out the door.

I leave Andi an e-mail, vaguely explaining that I might be out of the loop for a day or two. Knowledge is not always good. Why worry about what you can't stop anyhow?

Then it's off to the office.

* * *

. . . WHERE THINGS are, as usual, FUBAR.

Before I can gather Sarah and Wheelie for an update, Sally Velez meets me halfway to my desk.

"Sarah got carjacked last night, coming home from work," she says. "Well, not quite carjacked. She did get away. Half-jacked, I guess. He got the car."

There is a crowd over by Sarah's office. Even the Gold Dust Twins, Leighton and Callie Ann, not Sarah's biggest fans, are part of the hoverfest. As I approach the mob, Sarah is in the process of sending them all on their way, thanking them for their concern and assuring them that everything's fine.

Which it obviously isn't.

I step up as she's about to shut the door and maybe lock it. I block it with my foot and step inside, uninvited.

"What the fuck?" I ask.

"What the fuck do you think? That son of a bitch Gates!"

"Tell me."

She was getting out of her car at the house she and her husband-to-be are renting and plan to buy.

"I never saw him coming. He grabbed the keys, pushed me across the seat, and jumped in. If the passenger-side door had been locked, I don't think I'd have gotten out in time."

As it was, she scraped herself up pretty good rolling to the curb as Luther Gates took off with the car.

"You're sure it was him?"

"Hell, yes. I got a good look at him as he was trying to drag me back in."

They found the car early this morning ditched somewhere in the East End, trashed up pretty good.

"What about Gates?"

"Somehow he got away. I don't know if he had another car or what, but they haven't caught him. Goddammit!"

Sarah would rather eat rat poison than have anybody at the paper see her cry, but I can see that she's about to lose it.

Luther Gates, child molester, apparently still has it in for Sarah because she committed journalism on him.

The cops have promised to give her protection, which means driving by the house every now and then, I guess.

"It's like he's fixated on me," she says. "And I didn't even have a chance to take the damn gun out of my purse."

That's the way it usually happens, I tell her. You get a gun, and maybe you go shooting once or twice at the range, but it's not really part of your world, and you have about two seconds to think to pull your weapon out of your purse, take the safety off, and fire. And even then, you're as likely to shoot yourself as your target. It's why I don't like to carry one.

"And there's plenty of people who want to shoot me."

"You know I know how to use one," she says. "Next time I'll be better prepared. Jack's packing now too."

I warn her that Luther Gates has "Nothing to Lose" stamped on his forehead now, if he didn't already. Sex with kids, jumping bail, and attempted kidnapping. Quite a trifecta.

"He gets more dangerous every time he pulls this kind of crap."

We finally come around to my reason for being in so early this fine Friday the thirteenth.

"Oh, yeah. God, I'm sorry. I forgot all about that whole thing with Purity."

She escorts me to Wheelie's office. We all three agree that getting B.S. Stine, our current publisher, involved in this would only make matters worse. And Stine has his hands full with other matters, what with our building sold out from under us and our rumored change to a six-day-a-week operation. The smart money's still on Tuesday.

There isn't much I can write about what I'm telling Sarah and Wheelie, although I'm still holding out hope that I'll have a hell of a story eventually, assuming I'm around to write it.

Right now, about all I can do is keep writing bullshit pieces about the cops' ongoing investigation into the three murders.

I give them all the details about why I won't be available this evening for night police beat duty.

"And they're just going to let you walk up to that house, go in, and tell them you don't have the DVD, but that they'll have to come somewhere else with you to get it?" Sarah says. "Isn't that going to, like, piss them off?"

Probably, I concede, but they really want that DVD, and they're sure I really want that quarter-million dollars.

"They'll probably go along with it," I say, hopeful that this is the case. "I'll tell them that I didn't feel comfortable bringing it to a place I didn't know. Besides, if anything starts to go wrong, the feds have given me this nifty alarm button."

I show them the little cell-phone-like device.

"And they're how far away?" Wheelie asks.

I tell him.

"Well, here's hoping they don't drop the ball."

"Or the bad guys don't just shoot your ass out of sheer irritation," Sarah adds. "You aren't exactly dealing with brain surgeons here. Even if it's rational to keep you alive until they get the DVD, rational might not carry the day."

I tell them that I'm feeling lucky.

Sarah reminds me that I always seem to be feeling lucky, whether the facts justify it or not.

"I'm just an optimistic guy," I reply.

They think that maybe I ought to just go home and rest some instead of writing what I'm allowed to write about the latest in the Stick Davis-Whit Charles saga.

I tell them I'll sleep when I'm dead, which they don't seem to think is all that funny.

Nor do they laugh when I ask if our latest owner, the Grimm Group, has gotten around to dropping our life insurance policies.

❋ ❋ ❋

THE AFTERNOON and early evening go smoothly enough.

I meet my beloved for late lunch or early dinner at the Robin Inn at five and try to reassure her that I'm safely in the hands of the nation, state, and city's finest.

"And you're going to call me as soon as it's over," she says. She's staying at her sister's again tonight, and I promise that I will indeed call her and then join her there, unless it's OK for us to go back to the Prestwould, which would be an immeasurably better outcome.

She kisses me goodbye after I walk her to her car. She seems a little weepy, and I feel bad for putting her through this. I feel like I'm being sucked into a whirlpool, that I got too close and now there's nothing to do but ride it out.

"You don't get paid to do this shit," Cindy says.

Well, she's right, but who the hell else is going to do it? Possibly I'm just, as L.D. Jones so delicately puts it, a nosy-ass bastard. Maybe it would've been better if I hadn't heard about that missing iPad, hadn't remembered à la mode and Bumpass, hadn't hacked into Stick's iPad, hadn't found that damn DVD. Once I found the DVD, though, and saw what was on it, the die was cast.

"I know. I know," she says to my protestations that I'm just trying to be a good citizen. But she's not really buying it.

❋ ❋ ❋

Nobody else in the office really knows about my nine P.M. assignation, although some of my cohorts seem to sense that I'm not taking the night off to go clubbing.

Leighton Byrd has been assigned the task of writing about Sarah's carjacking incident. Leighton, who reminds me a lot of Ms. Goodnight when she was a cub reporter, still holds a grudge over Sarah telling her and Callie Ann to dress a bit less provocatively a year or so ago.

When I walk by Leighton's desk a bit later, though, she calls me over and tells me, out of earshot of the nearest fellow reporter twenty feet away, that Sarah is "one tough bitch," presumably referring to Sarah's reaction to her near kidnapping. I'm pretty sure she means it as a compliment.

"She can teach you some shit," I tell Leighton, who only nods. Hell, she'll probably be my boss someday, too, if I last long enough.

L.D. and one of the feds get me on the speakerphone in the conference room at seven to ensure that we are all on the same page. I try to make double damn sure that when and if I press that button, I won't be left there holding my dick in my hand. I am assured that this will not be the case.

The chief asks me if I really want to do this.

"We can get these guys eventually," he says, "one way or the other."

"Before they blow something up?" I ask.

"We've got your back," an FBI guy says, and I really want to believe him.

* * *

At 8:40, I take my leave.

"Be careful," Wheelie says when I stop by his office. He and Sarah intend to stay here until they hear from me. Yeah, they'll be my second call, right after Cindy.

He shakes my hand, which is somehow unnerving. Sarah follows me to the elevator.

"Here," she says, trying to press her lady pistol into my hand. "You need this more than I do."

I step back, unnerved again by the sight of a probably loaded weapon in our newsroom. I explain that I will surely be searched when I get to my destination, and that I'm not sure she doesn't need it more than I do anyhow, although it is my sincere belief that whatever happens to Luther Gates, he won't be brought to justice by her playing Annie Oakley.

We tell each other to be careful, then she presses my right hand in both of hers. The elevator dings, the door opens, and I'm gone.

I park the Honda right in front of the address I've been given. The house is a Cape Cod that looks like it was built sometime in the 1950s and needs a major makeover.

There are no lights inside, at least none that I can see. I check again to make sure I have the right address. I do.

I knock twice, and then my phone rings.

"Hey, asshole," the voice says, "there's been a change of plans."

Well, it isn't really a change of plans. It's more like these Purifiers aren't quite as dumb as they seem.

They don't appear to have sniffed out the fact that I'm being used as fed bait to lead them into a trap, but just in case, they're directing me to a second address, one they're not willing to share with me at present.

The voice informs me that they'll tell me where to go, that I have to keep my cell phone on, and they'll direct me. It seems like the wrong time to point out that the commonwealth of Virginia frowns on driving while talking on your cell phone.

When I protest these new arrangements, the voice says, "We just don't trust your ass, you bein' one of the mud people and all." I hear a snicker. God, I want to bust these fuckers. "You got the DVD, right?"

I hesitate for half a second and then tell them that I do, not quite sure where this is all headed.

"Just be sure you have the money," I reply.

"Oh, we got it all right," the voice says.

Then he warns me that I'm being watched, and that I'd better be damn sure nobody is following me. Who knows whether he's bullshitting me or not?

The Purity guy gives me the instructions again.

"Just keep your phone to your ear. We'll lead you to the promised land, black boy."

That special phone the feds gave me also allows them to monitor my calls. I can only hope they know what just transpired.

The idea of insisting that the Purifiers come with me to a different exchange location, back near Jordan's Branch where a welcoming party awaits them, seems kind of past due date now. Maybe I can work that out when we get to the undisclosed rendezvous.

I wonder if maybe I should just call it a night and get the hell out of Dodge.

I pull out of the parking space and head back toward Staples Mill Road. But before I have a chance to decide whether or not to follow the bad guy's instructions or just call and tell the feds to forget it, my fate is decided for me.

As I'm easing up to the stop sign, a car that was idling on the right side of the street does a forty-five-degree turn and blocks me.

Before I can do anything about that, like throw my Honda in reverse and get the fuck out of there, a large, bald man with a great big gun appears at my driver's side window. He grabs the car door and pulls it open before I can lock it.

I hear the passenger-side door open, and as I turn around, there's another goon. This one is a weird-looking dude who seems somewhat doped up. He's short and skinny and kind of wall-eyed, but he's equally well-armed. He slides in beside me.

"We thought you might need an escort," the guy at the door says, "just to make sure your ass doesn't get lost or something."

Then he goes back to the car that's blocking my way and gets in. The squirrelly little guy, who has a gun aimed at my head, tells me to follow. He doesn't seem open to negotiation.

Then he reaches down into the console and pulls out the cell phone.

"You won't be needin' this," he says in a wheezy voice, and he throws it out the window. He puts the gun back to my head.

"Drive," is all he says.

Fuck.

CHAPTER FOURTEEN

I'm directed down Staples Mill to Broad, where the guy with the gun orders me to go east. The other car, the one that blocked me, is following, as is a van I can see in the rearview mirror. My attempts to engage my captor in conversation are met with silence, other than his advice that I should "shut the fuck up," followed by a racial pejorative.

Then it's left on Roseneath and into Scott's Addition. We drive past Tazza Kitchen, one of my favorite joints. I briefly wonder if I'll ever get to order the white pizza with bacon bits again.

Just beyond Tazza, I am directed to turn right on Moore, then left on Mactavish, and then left again on Norfolk. Just past a strip club of my acquaintance, I'm ordered to turn into an alleyway between two buildings that haven't yet been converted from industrial use into hip housing and eateries.

The big guy comes around and pulls me from behind the wheel, then gags me. Two other bruisers get out of their car, some kind of retro-sixties gas guzzler, and they lead me along some cobblestone steps to what turns out to be the side door of a building I've probably passed a hundred times but never noticed before. The van eases in behind the second one, and another guy gets out.

Without the cell phone, I can only hope that our federal, state, and local cops have some idea where I am.

I'm dragged inside, then up a flight of stairs to a room that seems to take up most of the second floor. The place smells like dust and engine oil, with maybe a little urine thrown in.

The goon with the tattooed forehead sits me down in some kind of beat-up office chair. The little guy who directed me here stands to one side and the goon is on the other. The others stand behind them, with their arms folded. They take the gag off, and then they tie me to the chair.

I look around. The walls are festooned with Nazi and Confederate flags. Blinds have been drawn over all the outside windows.

"We got him," one of the assholes on the back row says. "Now what're we gonna do with him?"

Nobody says anything, although it doesn't take a mind reader to know that none of the options they're considering will make me very happy.

"Let me go," I suggest.

Tattoo man, who has been quiet, speaks.

"Not fuckin' likely," he says. The silence that follows makes me believe that this guy is the leader, the brains of the operation if there are any.

He pulls a chair up facing mine and straddles it. He's not a bad-looking dude, until you take a closer look. He is dressed a bit more neatly than his comrades, with jeans that look like they've been ironed, and a dress shirt. Unlike most of them, he doesn't seem to have subsisted on Big Macs and french fries for the last five years. He looks very fit, like he might be ex-military.

But his eyes are what tell you he's crazy as a bedbug. He blinks them once every minute or two, and they're black as a coal mine. Unlike my other captors, he doesn't have a scraggly-ass beard, but his mouth has a downward turn to it, like a smile would cause his face to break. Actually a beard might help his looks, because he has a raw, red scar running from near his ear almost to his lips. And there's the tattooed forehead.

"So, tell me," he says, speaking almost in a whisper, "how about that DVD?"

I explain that I don't have it.

"I didn't trust you. I planned to have you follow me to another location, where I felt safer."

The guy doesn't say anything at first.

"Well," he offers when he finally speaks, "that's OK, because we don't have a goddamn quarter of a million dollars to give your nigger ass either. We just thought you might be stupid enough to, ah, accept our invitation. We were just going to take the DVD and get rid of you."

"Let's just kill him, Randall," the little wheezy guy says. I notice that he seems to be doodling on a notepad of some kind, like he's the damn recording secretary or something.

"Shut up, Bug," Randall says. He seems irritated, maybe because I'm not supposed to know his name. "If we kill him now, we don't get the damn DVD, do we?"

Randall turns back to me.

"We aren't fuckin' around here," he says. "You need to tell us where that disc is. I know you saw what happened to ol' Whit. We don't want to make it hard on you. We just want what's ours, get me?"

He reaches behind him and pulls a big-ass gun from the waist of his jeans. He holds it a few inches from my face.

"Now that we understand each other," he says, "how about making it easy on yourself. Where. Is. That. Fucking. DVD?"

He says each word a little louder than the one before.

For lack of any better plan, I tell him that I've left the disc with a couple of friends, and that they are waiting for me to show up so we can make an exchange.

Randall smiles, and I wish he hadn't. His front four teeth seem to have been filed down to points, and they are all embedded with red letters. H-E-I-L, same as the spelling on his forehead. That smile, which goes no farther up than his upper lip, makes me wish even more for the arrival of the cavalry.

"And I'll bet they're all armed," he whispers as he moves so close I'm afraid he's going to bite me.

"That was the plan. We didn't trust you to just hand over the money."

"Good point," Randall says. "But you didn't count on our little ambush, did you?"

I have to concede that I didn't.

"Look," I tell him, "come with me and I'll lead you to it. My friends don't know anything about what's on the DVD. They just know I need backup."

The guy shakes his head.

"Uh-uh. Bullshit on you. No way in hell you didn't blab something about this to your so-called friends. You shoulda kept your big mouth shut."

"And just let you kill my ass?"

Randall displays the world's most unpleasant smile again.

"Well, yeah, there is that."

He retreats, and the others follow him, far enough away that I can't hear what they're saying, or most of it at any rate.

I hear bits and pieces of sentences as the Purity geniuses try to figure out their next move. ". . . got to get that disc," I hear, and some discussion about ". . . got to do them all," and plans to dump somebody or bodies somewhere.

"OK," Randall says. "Your lucky day. We're not going to kill you. Just tell us where your friends are, and we'll go and get that DVD. But you better not be lying about this. Remember ol' Whit."

Who could forget? Since there are no friends out there holding on to the disc, unless you count the cops as my friends, I need to make something up, something that will at least buy me a little time.

I figure that the authorities probably have already scrambled from what was supposed to be their command headquarters for this totally fucked-up operation, but maybe they're still around, although they shouldn't be. They should be tearing Richmond apart looking for the guys who somehow managed to spirit me away from right under their noses.

Maybe, though, I can send these goons over there and I'll get lucky. At most, it will keep me alive a little longer. If they come back empty-handed, it'll probably be time for them to start playing "this little piggy" with my fingers and toes. So I give them the address where the cops were ensconced.

I am smart enough to know that, should they get their hands on that DVD, I've smoked my last Camel, but maybe the cops are still there and will take these guys out before they take me out.

"Your so-called friends probably have already left by now," Randall says, shaking his head. He walks over to me and grabs me by the throat, depriving me of oxygen for what seems like a very long time.

"Tell me," he says, "how long were they going to wait for you to show up?"

He lets go long enough for me to tell him that the plan was to stay as long as it took.

He squeezes again. I'm afraid he's going to crush my windpipe, but he lets go finally.

"OK," he says.

He calls the other Purifiers over and tells them where they're supposed to go to pick up the DVD.

"But we ain't got no money," the one called Bug whines, looking up from whatever the fuck he's doodling.

"Of course we ain't got no money, you idiot," Randall says. "We didn't ever have any money. You're supposed to get the disc and take care of this asshole's so-called friends."

Everybody seems to know what that means.

Randall says he'll stay here and make sure I don't manage to untie myself and escape.

The others leave.

"I guess it's just you and me then," he says after they've gone. He grins.

I figure it won't take them more than half an hour to get back to the address I gave them off Staples Mill, where they'll either find an empty house or have one hell of a shootout with the cops.

On the off chance that I see daylight again, I try to get a little information out of Randall.

"What are you planning to do?"

He scratches himself with that big-ass gun.

"Well," he says, "I don't want to say much, even though I doubt you're ever going to be able to tell anybody. Hell, I'm just keepin' you alive to see whether you've told the truth or not. Might decide how we kill you."

And so he tells me a story.

CHAPTER FIFTEEN

The Stick Davis I knew was no hero, but it seems like he did plan to do at least one semi-heroic thing in his sorry-ass life.

From what my captor tells me, Stick acted as if he was kind of taken with his new Purity pals down in the islands.

"He knew some of us were from Virginia," Randall tells me. "We hooked up with him at this bar we all liked to go to, up on this little mountain in the middle of the island. Wasn't anybody much up there to bother us, not so many mud people around like there was down below."

Stick had been in Virgin Gorda for about four months, the best I can do the math, when he started hanging around with these creeps.

"He seemed like he was all in," Randall says. He has a pint of Jim Beam with him, and he's nursing it.

He seems hurt by Stick's betrayal, even though he and his cronies have settled my old pal's hash pretty good already. "I mean, he said all the right things, about how we had to stop the niggers and the spicks from taking over the country and all."

He doesn't bother to say "no offense."

I don't deny that Stick Davis had few redeeming qualities, unless he developed them well into his adulthood.

However, it never seemed to me that he was a bone-deep racist. It doesn't jibe with anything we did, drunk or sober, back in the day, and it doesn't mesh with anything he said to me when we were trying to ghostwrite his memoirs. I mean, he did choose a guy with an African American father to write them.

"I suppose, if we had known he used to hang out with the likes of a half-breed like you," my captor says, "we might have suspected that the bastard was a traitor."

Apparently the Purifiers were happy enough with Stick to make him privy to their unholy plans.

"He knew all about what we did in Charlottesville, and he acted like he thought it was kind of cool. And he knew what we were planning next."

He doesn't say what the "what" is. I figure he'll get around to it.

"There's plenty more of us," he says, "and when we make our little statement, they'll come out of the woodwork. Then you'll see what kind of country this is."

Yeah, I think, that's what I'm afraid of.

While Stick was working for Whit Charles and generally having a fine old time getting stoned and banging teenagers, he also was going to meetings with his new buddies in rooms that no doubt were festooned with the same kind of flags I'm looking at now.

The Purity gang knew Charles, through Stick.

"I think that he might've known something was goin' on, but Stick said he was cool, or at least dumb."

I ask Randall about the DVD.

He frowns.

"I hate a fuckin' thief," he says.

We all have our standards. Some people hate thieves. Some people hate bigots.

The Purifiers had been making plans for some time when Stick didn't show up for one of their meetings. That was about a year ago, not long before he popped up back here in Richmond.

It wasn't until the next week that somebody realized that something was missing.

"We'd made this DVD," Randall says. "I suppose you've already seen it, so you know what it's about. We've made several copies, and we're going to mail them to the governor, both senators, the newspapers, so they'll know what we did after we do it. So they know they can't fuck with us like they did in Charlottesville.

"So you see why we didn't exactly want ol' Stick tipping everybody's hand, spoiling our party."

"How did you know he'd taken the DVD?"

"It was gone, and he was gone. We ain't stupid. We also heard rumors that he'd stolen a bunch of money from Whit Charles. We figured he'd gone back to the States, and we knew he was from Richmond."

They had those other copies, of course, but they knew they had to make sure the one Stick stole didn't fall into the cops' hands and tip everybody off.

The Purifiers thought maybe Stick had just decided to forget all about them.

"But then we got this letter."

Stick wanted money in exchange for the DVD.

"He was an idiot. He said he wanted fifty thousand dollars for it, or he'd give it to the fuckin' feds."

Randall laughs.

"Hell, you drove a harder bargain than he did, although it didn't turn out so good for you either, did it?"

I have more important things to worry about than Stick Davis's motives, like how I'm going to keep breathing awhile longer, but the whole thing does intrigue me.

"We knew we had to do something," Randall says. "It was time to come north anyhow."

He pokes the gun in my face.

"So you're the goddamn Shakespeare who was going to help make Stick Davis famous."

I hasten to assure the guy that Stick didn't reveal anything more to me than what the Purifiers have already gleaned from the pages they took. Even to me, it sounds like bullshit.

"Well," Randall says, "I don't guess it matters much whether you knew what he was up to or not. Your ass won't be around to see how it's all going to end. Suffice it to say that it won't be a happy ending, not for you and your kind anyhow."

It didn't take Sherlock Holmes to find Stick. Once the bad guys figured out where he was, they packed up and came back to the States.

"It was almost time anyhow," Randall says. "Oops. Don't want to give that away, even if dead men don't tell any fuckin' tales."

The two Purity members charged with ensuring that Stick didn't give away their plans broke in that Friday while their prey was out drinking and waited for him. They used suppressors to keep the neighbors from hearing.

"But the numb nuts didn't get the DVD," Randall says, shaking his head. "They got the damn book, or the part you'd written, but who gives a shit about that? They got a little too enthusiastic and killed Stick before they could get him to tell them where the disc was. Then when I came Sunday, it wasn't there."

When the Purifiers couldn't find the disc they so badly wanted, they tried to figure out who Stick might have shared it with.

They found out that Whit Charles had come back to Virginia for the funeral, and they thought he might be in on whatever Stick was cooking up.

My captor says they knew about the place where I met Charles out near Zion Crossroads.

"We followed him out there the day you and him met," he says, "but nobody stuck around long enough for us to do the deed then."

He laughs.

"Shame, because we could have taken care of the whole damn bunch of you right there. Instead we had to ambush him and that damn bodyguard, whatever, at the house he was staying at.

"But he couldn't tell us nothin,' and believe me, if he'd known, he'd of told us, by the time we got through with him.

"And so that left us with you. And when you tried to shake us down, well, that's why you're in the fix you're in right now."

Where the fuck, I'm wondering, are the cops?

I have two pressing needs right now. I could use a cigarette, and I have to piss like a racehorse.

I ask for the Camel first. My captor is kind enough to take one out of my pocket. I figure that by the time I've smoked it down to the nub, my number will be up.

"Can't deny a dying man his last wish," Randall says, taking a swig from the pint. "Do you want a blindfold too?"

He seems to think that's funny.

So he puts the cigarette in my mouth, lights it, and I puff away, not much concerned any more about the possibility of future lung cancer. Cindy, Peggy, and everyone else who's warned me about the perils of puffing can rest assured that, in the end, my lungs weren't the problem. It's always the thing you don't count on that gets your ass.

When I inquire about taking a leak, Randall is a little less charitable, suggesting that I probably won't be needing my present pair of trousers much longer anyhow.

My request seems to trigger my captor's urinary urges though.

"I'll be right back," he tells me. "Now don't go anywhere."

He's cracking himself up.

The bathroom seems to be at the far end of the building. Randall wanders in that direction, pint bottle and gun in hand.

My captors haven't gone to extreme lengths to keep me immobilized. Duct tape secures my legs to the chair, and plastic ties bind my arms behind me.

The good news: I can tell that the ties aren't connected to the back of the chair.

There are very few advantages to being double-jointed. It can make for amusing demonstrations, and it always tickles my grandson, young William, when grandpa can bend his thumbs all the way back to his wrists. Andi isn't happy that I've shown her son that particular trick, because he keeps trying to do it himself, which, not being double-jointed, he can't.

There's another thing old double-jointed Willie can do that probably didn't occur to the goddamn Purifiers.

If the twist ties have enough leeway, I can clasp my hands behind my back and lift them over my head—which I am relieved to find that I can do as soon as Randall walks into the bathroom, which must be at least one hundred feet away.

Randall, not being the shy type, leaves the bathroom door open, but I can't see him, so he can't see me.

I spit out the cigarette.

The other slim hope in my arsenal lies in front of me. The Purity boys have been a little sloppy, and there are pieces of broken beer bottles on the floor not two feet away.

I very quietly lean forward, still attached to the chair at my ankles, until I'm on my knees. I am able to grab a piece of glass, maybe two inches across, and heave myself back up. And I start sawing.

Randall is still in the bathroom, either taking a very long piss or maybe, as long as he's there, going for number two also. At any rate, I'm sawing like a bastard, trying to free my right wrist with my left thumb and forefinger. I draw blood, but somehow that doesn't seem to be a big issue right now.

The tie goes pop just as I hear the toilet flush. I'm still duct-taped to a goddamn chair though.

One thing occurred to me, however, as I was moving back and forth in it: The damn chair is rickety as hell. I could feel it trying to give way.

Something makes me recall Bones MacNelly. Bones was a regular at the Chuck Wagon back when Oregon Hill had places like that, joints where you could find a whole set of teeth scattered about the parking lot after a particularly enthusiastic Saturday night.

Bones was called Bones much in the same way Australians sometimes nickname redheads "Blue." He weighed well on the far side of three hundred pounds.

One night when I was barely old enough to buy beer, Bones was at the Chuck Wagon, in his usual seat. He started complaining that his chair was, in his words, a piece of shit.

"It's all wobbly," he said.

The manager begged to differ, offended that someone was casting aspersions on his establishment's furniture. He suggested that perhaps the chair had not been well-served by having Bones's fat ass weighing down on it every night.

"I'll show you what a piece of shit it is," Bones said.

He lifted his butt up a few inches and slammed down, more or less turning the offending chair into firewood.

I don't weigh but about half what Bones did, but it's worth a try. And I'm out of alternative fucking ideas.

Randall is starting to head back my way. All I've accomplished so far will just piss the Purifiers off if they catch me, but I do have that little piece of broken beer bottle in my hands, and I do have my last hope, inspired by Bones MacNelly.

I put my hands back behind my back, hoping my captor won't notice the splotch of blood among the broken glass and the smoldering cigarette butt on the dirty floor in front of me.

"Peed your pants yet?" Randall asks, throwing in the obligatory racist slur. Still the comedian. He's zipping up as he walks back in my direction. He sets the gun down on the floor beside him.

When he checks his cell phone to see if he's heard anything yet from his fellow goons, I try to make the most out of the only chance I can see.

Randall doesn't seem to understand what's happening when I lift myself out of the chair as high as I can with my arms still behind me. He starts to say something, no doubt humorous, possibly about my unrequited need to urinate, when I slam back down as hard as I can.

The first time, the chair starts breaking apart. One leg falls off, and I can feel the seat starting to separate from the other legs.

On the second try, the whole thing just turns to splinters, allowing me to stand. The chair legs to which my own are duct-taped are now independent of each other.

Randall, maybe because he's drunk most of that pint already, is a little slower than he might have been in reaching for the gun on the floor beside him. And he's a tad surprised when he sees that my hands are also free. He doesn't notice the piece of glass until I've managed to give him what I hope is a very nasty cut on his right arm.

When he grabs his arm and falls to his knees, I move a few steps forward and kick the damn gun as far as I can. It goes sliding across the pine floor, halfway to the bathroom.

As I try to get around Randall and head in the general direction of freedom, he reaches for my right leg. I kick him in the face as hard as I can and run for it, the two chair legs still attached to my taped ankles, banging against the wood floor.

I probably have a twenty-foot head start. I'm no sprinter, but desperation makes Usain Bolts of us all. Stumbling and bumbling down the stairs in my semi-shackled state, I expect to hear Randall behind me, but I hear nothing, and it occurs to me that he must have decided to go back and get his bang-bang before pursuing me farther.

Seldom has air smelled as sweet as what hits me when I burst out the door.

And there, the next building down, is that strip club from my tomcatting days, its neon sign no less welcoming than a lighthouse to a storm-tossed sailor.

I run in the front door. There's a cover charge, the fat guy at the counter says. Then he looks at me and decides that maybe I'm not gentlemanly enough for a gentlemen's club, what with my bleeding hand, plastic ties hanging from both wrists, and part of what once was a chair taped to my ankles.

I manage to get past the "what the fucks" and explain to the guy that there's a man with a gun who might be coming in the door presently, looking for me.

This encourages him to call 911 and get out his own weapon. In the meantime, it appears that Randall has decided to go in another direction than the front door of the Pussycat Lounge.

I borrow a phone from a bystander who finds me more interesting than the winsome ladies making love to the pole in the next room.

L.D. answers after the first ring.

"Man," he says, "where are you?"

I tell him, and then I ask him where the fuck he and the Keystone Kops have been.

The chief tries to explain how it happened, but I'm not in the mood. I suggest that he get his ass over here now. When he seems to take umbrage at my attitude, I further suggest he engage in sexual self-gratification.

Then I hang up.

"Dude," the guy says when I give him back his phone, "you've pissed your pants."

CHAPTER SIXTEEN

Saturday, September 14

It is somewhat difficult to believe that I am sitting here in Joe's Inn, surrounded by family (well, Cindy) and friends. Less than twelve hours ago, I was tied to a chair in an abandoned warehouse, wondering if I was smoking my last cigarette. My adventures of late necessitated a special Saturday morning meeting of the Oregon Hill Breakfast Club.

There's a bodyguard with a big-ass gun sitting next to me.

"Dude," R.P. McGonnigal says, "you've got more lives than a damn cat."

❋ ❋ ❋

THE COPS got to the strip club no more than five minutes after I called the chief to tell him that, no thanks to him, I was still among the living. There were so many blue lights and government cars that the crowd inside must have thought it was a drug bust.

Somebody had already found a bandage, and the Good Samaritan and his helpers had more or less dealt with the beer-bottle cut I gave myself sawing my way to freedom. They even helped me get free from the damn duct tape connecting my legs to remnants of the chair. Before the police arrived, I had time to slip into a room and remove my soggy underwear, somewhat easing my discomfort.

During all this excitement, there was no sign of Randall or any of the other Purifiers. The linebacker guarding the entrance had a rather impressive gun in his right hand just in case.

The cops, when they got there, took their sweet time entering the building I'd escaped from.

"It might be booby-trapped or something," one of the feds explained. He scowled when I observed that I wished they had shown as much concern for my well-being as they displayed for their own.

Finally the cops went inside. By that time, it was after midnight. The strip-club crowd was mostly hanging around alfresco, behind the yellow tape that had been hastily put up. The onlookers seemed disappointed when no gunfire emanated from the warehouse.

"Shit," I heard one of them say, "now the club's closed for the night, and they didn't even shoot nobody."

"No boobs and no bodies," somebody added.

When it seemed that there was no sign of my captor, they led me into the building so I could give them a guided tour. I showed them the big room on the second floor and described my evening. They didn't appear to mind when I lit up a Camel. I noticed that my hands were not as steady as they might have been.

They seemed impressed that I was still alive.

"Man," L.D. said, "we thought we'd lost you." His sincerity almost allowed me to forgive him.

I replied that they did lose me, somewhere off Staples Mill Road.

There didn't seem to be much left in the way of evidence in the room, other than a large collection of hate literature, some flags that needed burning, and a sizable collection of skin mags.

I'm sure there's DNA galore to help the authorities eventually catch these bastards. The question, though, is whether they can catch them before they do whatever they're planning to do.

And, I'm happy to say, there was a goodly amount of Randall's blood soaking into the wooden floor.

"We know who these fuckers are," one of the feds said. "We didn't know where they'd gone to. Now we know."

It would be better, I suggested, if they knew where the fuck they were right now.

"We're on that," he assured me. These government guys might screw up royally, but they don't lack for confidence.

The man who was guarding me, I was told, is one Randall Heil, which would explain the attractive forehead tattoo. He's an ex-con and a big star in the Nazi and Klan circuit.

"He changed his name," the fed said. "We don't know much about him, except that his real name, his birth name, is supposed to be Randall Herrmann."

I told the cops about being abducted from under their damn noses and tried to describe the other vehicles—the one that followed my captor and me to the warehouse, and the van. I remember the one that blocked me. Big-old muscle car, might have been a GTO. Dark blue, rag top. I showed them where the car had been parked next to mine.

"Shouldn't be that hard to find," one of the state guys muttered. Yeah, I was thinking but not saying, easy for somebody who can find his ass with both hands.

It became pretty obvious that Randall Heil, or whatever the fuck his name was, had decided that his best bet was to grab his gun and get the hell out of Dodge.

My car was sitting by its lonesome on the side of the building.

I had what I thought was a pretty pertinent question for the chief and his posse.

"What the fuck happened?"

The way they explained it:

The feds were all ready in their little stakeout two blocks away when I was ambushed on Franklin. When my lifeline phone was thrown out the window, they apparently didn't know anything was wrong at first. When they didn't hear anything for about a minute and the phone wasn't moving, they said they took off for the Airbnb house.

By then, my escorts and I were headed in the opposite direction, down Staples Mill and toward the warehouse where I nearly cashed in on that company life insurance policy.

"We didn't know what kind of car they had or anything," L.D. said. "We just knew that you weren't there."

They knew I was driving a Honda Accord, but who the fuck isn't? By all accounts, they were looking all over hell and creation for me, everywhere, it seems, except in one warehouse in Scott's Addition.

I did my best to describe the other skinheads.

When the dust finally settled, it was suggested that I might need some protection. They gave me back my original cell phone, and I called Cindy.

I explained to her that I would have to spend at least one more night at another location. My beloved, who had not yet been to bed as she waited for my call, wanted to know why, and I tried to tell her about my night, leaving out some of the more exciting parts. It is hard, though, to make an abduction sound like anything but an abduction.

"They kidnapped your ass?" she said.

But I got away, I explained. It's all good.

I told Cindy that it would be smarter all around if I let the feds take me to a nice, safe, well-guarded hotel until they catch these fuckers.

"I don't want you in some damn hotel," Cindy whined. "I want you here."

Soon enough, I told her, with fingers crossed.

❊ ❊ ❊

LAST NIGHT'S insanity was over a bit late to make the Saturday paper.

However, I did give our online readers a taste. The feds didn't want me to write anything about their "ongoing investigation," but I insisted. Considering their track record in keeping me out of harm's way, they knew they did not hold the moral high ground.

So I spilled such information as I had so far and posted it. I also called Sarah Goodnight, who was still in the office at one A.M., waiting to hear from me.

"Wait. Wait," she interrupted. "You got kidnapped, and you escaped? What the hell, Willie?"

I explained that I didn't mean to get kidnapped. It just kind of happened.

She did seem glad to hear from me though. She bemoaned the fact that I'd managed to get away too late to get anything into the paper. I promised to escape more quickly next time.

There is, however, an extensive report on my goings and comings last night out there in the ether. Writing for the website means never having to have your copy cut.

The bottom line, information that has already been picked up by every media outlet in the state, is that there are some bad guys still at large who want to make a lot of noise, but the cops don't know where or when.

I did try, after my escape, to get somebody on the federal, state, or local level to comment on the "ongoing investigation," but, being an "ongoing investigation," nobody had anything to say.

❊ ❊ ❊

THIS MORNING, the sun was shining in my room at the Omni. I told my bodyguard that I wanted to go to breakfast. He said he'd accompany me downstairs. I told him, no, I want to go to Joe's.

He was not happy with that plan, but I stood my ground.

"You guys damn near got me killed," I explained. "Now I want to see my wife and maybe a few friends."

And so here we sit, R.P. and Brooklyn, Andy Peroni, Custalow, Cindy, and a mildly unhappy fed with a big-boy gun. He insisted on joining the party after I made my calls. We told him to go for the toast instead of the biscuit.

We've had to settle for a table in the other room at Joe's, our normal spot having been taken over by a horde of young folk, a couple of them in what appears to be their pajama pants.

The waitress seems surprised, though not overjoyed, to see us here on a Saturday. We tell her not to worry, that we'll be back tomorrow too.

"Lucky me," I hear her mutter.

R.P. and Brooklyn seem to take a proprietary interest in my recent adventures, having given me shelter.

"We might of been killed or something," Brooklyn says.

Close, I tell him, speaking from experience, doesn't count.

Abe, who has spent the last couple of nights at the apartment of local rock diva Stella Stellar, wants to know if it's safe for him to return to the Prestwould.

My bodyguard says it might be a good idea to give it another day or so "at least until we catch these guys."

I have a second opinion, which I'll impart to the guy after breakfast.

I'm not quite so cautious, noting that it seems to me that the Purifiers have bigger problems than old Willie right now, like how to avoid what has become at least a statewide manhunt.

"I wish those guys would have tried some shit like that up on the Hill, back in the day," Andy says.

Cindy, his sister, reminds him that, back in the day, there were plenty of guys in our lily-white neighborhood who would have been Purifier material. She's right. Custalow and I were about the only blemishes on the alabaster demographic of Oregon Hill back then, and there were some people who thought we were two minorities too many.

"Well," Andy says, "we weren't all like that."

Indeed, the little gang I hung with wasn't like that. R.P., Andy, Abe, the missing Goat Johnson, the late Sammy Samms, and I weren't saints, but we were better than that.

Sometime early into our third hour of hogging the table, as the bodyguard keeps looking at his watch and wondering, like our server, when the hell we're going to leave, I get a call.

Francis Xavier "Goat" Johnson has somehow heard about my recent adventures. He's calling from Ohio, where he inexplicably has not yet been fired as president of a college that obviously needs a search committee.

"What the fuck, Willie?" the academic component of our posse inquires.

I tell him where I am and who's with me and put him on speakerphone.

"You're there on a Saturday? Damn, the folks at Joe's must be bustin' their buttons over that."

"Joy is unrestrained," I hear our server say to one of her peers.

So I give Goat the quick version of what's transpired the last twenty-four hours.

"Man, you all have got some crazy human beings down there," he says. "First Charlottesville, and now this."

I point out that quite a few of the perpetrators of the neo-Nazi disgrace in C-ville were from elsewhere, including some from Ohio.

"Yeah," he says, "but they go down there to go batshit."

Goat catches up for five minutes or so and then hangs up. We show some mercy on our server and my bodyguard and finally pay the bill, leaving tips of as much as 20 percent.

"Don't be a stranger," our server says, but not like she means it.

After breakfast, I turn to my bodyguard and give him his walking papers.

"It's been swell," I tell him, "but now I want to go home."

He protests that it's his job to protect me.

Fine, I reply, but if you do it, you'll have to do it from the lobby of the Prestwould. Cindy and I need a little quiet time.

The bodyguard gets on the phone to his fed masters and, after a few intense minutes, hands the phone to me, so that I can assure whoever's on the other end that I'm taking responsibility for my own safety from now on.

I mean, how much worse can I screw that up than the cops have already?

Custalow says he'll come back later this afternoon.

When we get inside our unit (if, indeed, "our unit" is the right phrase for an apartment we are renting from my ex-wife), Cindy turns to me.

"I don't know whether to kick your ass or rip your clothes off," she says.

I express a preference for the latter, and she agrees, "although I might want to kick your ass later too."

* * *

I DO manage to crawl out of bed about one. Obviously there's a lot of typing to do before the Sunday edition goes to press tonight.

I've ignored a few phone calls in the interim, finally turning the damn thing off. Most of them, I see, are from my immediate bosses, Mal Wheelwright and Sarah.

I give Wheelie a quick call and tell him I'll be in the office in half an hour.

On the way out of the building, I am not surprised to run into Feldman in the lobby, where McGrumpy seems to live.

"Killed anybody today?" he asks. McGrumpy is, among other faults, irritatingly repetitive.

"Not yet," I reply, "but there are some really bad guys looking for me. If some big skinheads with guns come in here, tell them you haven't seen me."

On the off chance that I'm not pulling one of his aged legs, he heads for the elevator.

* * *

There aren't many people in the newsroom when I get in a little after two. Hell, there are never many people in the newsroom these days. Now that they're selling the building and seem intent on making us a less than daily publication, enthusiasm for going that extra mile and showing up unpaid on a Saturday has waned considerably.

The sports desk guys are watching a college game on TV. Two copy editors are feverishly trying to read everything that's going into the local section, a task that used to involve five or six of them. Leighton Byrd, still too young to have gone into complete fuck-this-shit mode, is working on a story.

I head over to Wheelie's office. Sarah sees me come in and meets me there. I am surprised when Leighton joins us.

After they congratulate me on being alive and writing something coherent for our free online readers, Wheelie moves on to the Sunday paper. You can win a Pulitzer

Prize on Saturday, and they want to know what you're going to do for Sunday.

Wheelie surprises me though.

"We thought it might be good," he says, clearing his throat the way he does when he has something difficult to say, "if, instead of having you write it first-hand again, maybe we ought to have another reporter interview you."

So now I know why Leighton is standing here with the grownups. She smiles in what I'm sure she hopes is an ingratiating manner.

"You think somebody else could tell it better than the guy who was in the chair?" I inquire, only raising my voice a little.

"Well," Wheelie says, "we just want it to be objective. You know, maybe you're too close to it."

"Too close to it?" I reply, perhaps upping the volume a bit. "Damn right I was too close to it. If I'd been any closer, Leighton would be writing my goddamn obit right now."

"Nobody's questioning your ability to write the story, Willie," Wheelie says. "But this might need a different approach."

I notice that Sarah isn't saying anything.

Hell, I have six messages on my phone from other news sources wanting me to tell them my story. As if. Everybody wants this story. But it's mine.

This doesn't make sense. And then the penny drops.

"This is B.S., isn't it?" I ask. They know I'm not talking about bullshit, although it's that too. I can feel the sweaty palms on Benson Stine, our present publisher, all over this one. And I know for a fact, or as factual as a report from Enos Jackson on the copy desk can be, that little Leighton has been seen in the company of our publisher at Lemaire's bar in the Hotel Jefferson, laughing at his stupid-ass jokes.

Nobody denies my assumption.

I flatly refuse to let Leighton Byrd or any other ambition addict tell my story. OK, I tell other people's stories all the time, but, goddammit, I'm the teller, not the tellee.

"It's what B.S. wants," Sarah says, rolling her eyes.

"If he wants the fucking story," I tell them all, "he's going to have to endure reading it with a Willie Black byline."

Then I do the adult thing and storm out, refusing to listen to what passes for reason.

Leighton, to her credit, does come to my desk and tell me it wasn't all her idea.

"It was just something Benson brought up," she says.

"Leighton," I tell her, "you have the makings of a really good journalist. Hell, if I last long enough, you'll probably be my boss one day. But you're poaching, and poaching's a felony in my book."

She turns to walk away.

I have one more bit of advice.

"Benson Stine won't be around here forever. We run through publishers like toilet paper. Don't hitch your fucking star to B.S."

She stomps off. At least she didn't cry.

Nobody else brings up the possibility of my being interviewed by my own newspaper. I see Wheelie in his office, the door closed, having an intense conversation with someone.

When he walks out half an hour later, he heads toward my desk. He doesn't stop, just says as he walks past, "Write it. Fuck it. Let him fire us all."

***

There's plenty to write. In addition to the whole kidnapping thing, it's time to give the readers a little background. I warn Sally Velez that this is going to be a stem-winder. It's time to tell the whole sad Stick Davis story, or as much of it as has played out so far.

I tell how the cops' suspicions turned from me to Jerome Sheets to parties unknown. I relate what I learned from Stick's neighbor about the mysterious strangers who came to the scene of the crime the day before the body was found and left with paper bags. I tell as much as I know about the luckless Whitney Charles.

I tell about how I accessed Stick's iPad and learned about the DVD that damn near got me killed. I relate more than L.D. or the feds want me to, I'm sure, about the botched plan to catch the Purifiers, and about my escape.

The lede, though, is what is likely to grab the attention of what few readers we have left.

"A neo-Nazi group that had a hand in the Charlottesville 'Unite the Right' fiasco in 2017 has returned. According to a video recording, the group, Purity, plans to wreak more havoc on Virginia sometime in the near future. The problem is, law authorities don't know where, and they don't know when."

Of course, as any sportswriter who has written the top to his game story with two minutes left only to see the home team blow an eight-point lead and lose at the buzzer can tell you, don't write your lede too early.

It's close to six when I get the call. I spoke with L.D. a couple of hours ago, not because I thought he'd tell me anything, but just to make sure that he knew his forces, the state guys, and the feds were going to be wearing a bit of egg on their faces tomorrow morning. He cursed me a bit, but his heart really wasn't in it. It's been a bad week for the chief.

"Just go easy," were his final words. It was about as chagrined as I've ever heard L.D. I almost felt sorry for my old gym-rat buddy.

So I figured he was calling this time to make one last pitch for a little mercy from the fourth estate.

But that wasn't it.

"We thought you ought to know this," he said. "We think we know when they're going to do it."

Of all unlikely things, the brainstorm that solved that riddle sprang from the normally storm-free brain of Chauncey Gillespie.

My donut-eating sometimes source on the police force remembered something.

Randall Heil's real last name, Herrmann, caused something to click with Gillespie.

He remembered reading about a shootout that happened five years ago in Idaho. A bunch of skinheads refused to vacate a shack on somebody else's property. Before it was over, federal agents were fired on and, surprise, fired back. Final tally: One less skinhead.

The story wouldn't have been more than a short in the B section, except that the victim, Roger Herrmann, was from one of those soulless suburbs in Northern Virginia. I vaguely remember that we ran it inside the A section.

The cops, of course, knew what Randall Heil's name was before he changed it. So Gillespie accessed the write-up in the *Washington Post* and found a quote from the deceased's brother, who gave his name as Randall Herrmann.

In the interview, Randall went on at length about the "murder" of his brother, which turned into a rant about law enforcement, government, and the United States in general.

"We will not forget this," Randall "Herrmann" is quoted as saying "Blood for blood."

Randall made enough noise that he got his picture in the *Post*.

If it isn't Randall Heil, it's his identical twin.

"So this is interesting," I say, humoring the chief, "but what's the importance?"

"The importance," L.D. says, "is the date. Roger Herrmann was shot and killed on September 16, 2014, five years ago."

I look at my calendar. Today's the fourteenth.

"Now," the chief says, "all we have to do is find the sons of bitches and figure out what they plan to blow up."

So, the smart money's on the sixteenth, two days away. I thank L.D. and tell him this is information our readers need to know.

"Yeah, I figured so," he said. "Otherwise, I'd never give you this kind of information. Don't get used to it."

"And you say Gillespie came up with this?"

I hear the chief chuckle.

"Blind hog finds acorn. But don't quote me on that."

There's plenty of time to rewrite the top of the story, telling our readers why the day after tomorrow might be a good day to watch out for suspicious packages.

We have a pretty likely answer to "when." The "where," though, is still a mystery, and apparently the cops have less than two days to answer that one.

Since the Purifiers are in our backyard, and based on what Heil told me when he thought I wouldn't be around to tell anybody else, this is going to be our story.

Here's hoping for a happy ending.

CHAPTER SEVENTEEN

Sunday, September 15

My deathless prose jumps twice in the Sunday morning paper, from A1 to A8 and then across to A9. At one time, not so long ago, this would have been a problem. Newsprint was finite and expensive.

It's no big deal these days. We don't have as much space to fill as we used to, but we damn sure don't have enough reporters to fill what we do have. I heard an assistant city editor the other day ask a reporter if she couldn't pad her story out another ten inches or so.

The whole damn A section is mostly crime news, fluff pieces promoting anything the paper can come up with to make money (meet local authors, come to our food festival, listen to great minds tell you how great they are; only seventy-five dollars a head if you act now), and furniture ads. We in the fourth estate are grateful that people still actually look at newspaper ads when they get the urge for a sofa.

So when you have a piece that tells the readers we have some bona fide nut jobs in our vicinity planning to blow something up tomorrow, but nobody knows what or where, you get the green light. Sky's the limit.

There is a sidebar quoting the governor and the mayor and the chief, telling people to be alert and maybe be cautious of suspicious packages. Leighton wrote that one. I have to say, she did a pretty good job. She managed to get some trenchant people-on-the-street stuff.

"I bet it's them ISIS bastards," one well-read individual said when approached outside a club down in the Bottom. Informed that the suspects are almost certainly red-blooded American neo-Nazis, the idiot took it in for a couple of seconds and then said, "Aw, that's just fake news."

We ran the photo of Randall Heil that appeared in the *Post* five years ago, and he hasn't changed that much, so he shouldn't be that hard to find, although he has added the tattoo since then. We put it on the web last night, and within an hour we'd had two people call us, sure they'd spotted the bastard. When I called L.D. at headquarters, he said they'd had leads from at least a dozen sharp-eyed citizens, none of which checked out.

"They damn near had a riot down at Poe's Pub," he said. "Some guys from one motorcycle club thought this asshole from another club sitting there drinking at the bar was Randall Heil."

The "discussion" spilled out onto East Main, where a hapless driver in an SUV coming in from a hard day bicycling on the Capitol Trail hit one of the participants and broke the guy's hip.

I tipped off Chuck Apple, who's subbing for me on night cops. I was thankful to let someone else handle that bit of mayhem.

He came by later and said he'd determined that nobody was killed or even near death.

"Fuck it then," Sally said. You've got to at least come close to killing somebody to make the paper, even with our present lax standards for what constitutes news. If it's an accident, Sally says, it has to be a fatality to get in the paper. If it's intentional, we sometimes let close calls count, but a broken hip stemming from a bar fight doesn't make the grade.

Long story short, the whole town's on edge. I ran the transcript of what was said on the DVD, so it's like we're waiting for a tornado, but we don't know where it's going to hit.

The governor has stationed guards around the capitol, one of our most stately and precious edifices. The place is already pretty well protected, as are most public buildings since 9/11, and the federal courts building and bank are even more impregnable than before.

Still, you can't guard everything.

"Maybe they just decided to go underground," R.P. suggested at brunch this morning.

Stella Stellar, who is back in town and came with Custalow, disagreed.

"Those bastards, they ain't giving up that easy."

There was a division of sentiment among the others at Joe's. People at adjoining tables wanted to join in on the discussion, which caused our server to threaten to banish us if the crowd around us didn't get the hell out of the way.

"Well," Andy said, "at least you got them reading the paper."

Yeah, that's the sad truth. You want people to buy a damn newspaper, scare the shit out of them or piss them off. Fear and anger sell. All those feel-good stories we run on A1 make everybody feel all warm and fuzzy, but there isn't much shelf life to a story about the guy who saved a pit bull from drowning, unless it's your pit bull.

I am paid to agitate people. Granted, there's plenty to get agitated about, but it does get wearisome, to say nothing of damn dangerous, to be the bearer of bad news, especially when "shoot the messenger" is not an abstraction.

The feds and the locals aren't saying much, because they don't have much to say. They did find that damn muscle car, abandoned on a street not far from Jordan's Branch, but there wasn't much in it that was of any use. They've identified Randall Heil and at least three of the other Purifiers, but finding them is another thing entirely.

When I told the assembled multitude that I had a meeting with some guys with guns at noon, we curtailed our second consecutive brunch day at Joe's, limiting it to Bloody Marys and coffee.

"That's OK," R.P. said. "You can't order the breakfast sandwich but so many times before it gets tiresome."

* * *

I DROP Cindy and Abe back at the Prestwould. Stella Stellar has to go back to her place and pack for another gig. The Goldfish Crackers are hitting the road again, albeit mostly two-lane state highways.

"Big doings," she says. "We're playing Farmville and Bedford on consecutive nights."

When I get to police headquarters, the place is humming. Nothing puts the fear of God into law enforcement more than the prospect of knowing bad shit is coming and they don't know where.

They're checking everybody who looks like he might ever have had a hard-on for Hitler or Jefferson Davis. Hell, yesterday they even shook down those old guys who pester everybody outside the Virginia Museum with their Confederate flags on Saturdays. Most of them look like they really *are* sons of Confederate veterans. Some of them have trouble lifting the flags.

"We think we have them on the run," the FBI guy says. "We can't see how they could possibly do anything now."

Sad to say, but I'm inclined to think Stella Stellar has a better bead on the situation than this J. Edgar wannabe. I mean, we know all the places the Purifiers aren't, but we sure as hell don't know where they are.

"We're pretty sure the Civil War monuments are safe," the chief says, in a rare display of humor that seems to be wasted on the feds.

I point out that the DVD meant for future dissemination said Purity had inflicted mayhem on Virginia, not just the city of Richmond.

"Well, we've got people on the lookout everywhere," one of the state police guys says.

On the wall calendar behind the chief, there's a big red circle around the sixteenth. Less than twelve hours from now.

They've included me in this tea party because I've obviously crossed the line and become part of the story. I didn't plan it that way, but I've been hip deep in this mess since I found Stick Davis's body. Sometimes you just get swept out with the news tide.

Everything that's discussed today is, of course, off the record, at least until they either do or don't catch the Purifiers before they wreak hell on us.

An hour or so of this and I'm ready to move on. One thing I've been meaning to do the last few days is revisit Terri McAllister. It might occur to the Purifiers that Stick could have told his last girlfriend something about their plans, although I'm not sure even Stick knew all the details.

She's at home, and she agrees to let me in.

She has spent the morning slinging hash at another of the seven million places that do brunch in Richmond. I am not sure the grocery stores even sell eggs to civilians anymore.

"That was some crazy shit," she says, referencing my story in today's paper. "It blows my fuckin' mind that Stick was hanging out with those creeps down there in the islands. He just didn't seem like that kind of guy."

I tell her that it's possible Stick was on the side of the angels, that he meant to blow the whistle on the Purifiers, in good time, while trying to make a buck out of the deal with his ill-fated tell-all.

"He did hide that disc, and tell me how to find it, eventually. If it wasn't for that, nobody would have had a clue about any of this," I tell her.

"Well, I'd like to think that ol' Stick had a heart of gold and all that."

I tell her that we should think of him that way at least.

She says that she never heard Stick say anything that might have indicated that he knew what exactly his island buddies were planning.

"If he'd known for sure, I don't think he'd of kept it a secret."

I'm not sure. Apparently Stick seems to have been pretty good at keeping secrets.

I call in to the newsroom from my parking spot on Floyd Avenue, to advise that I'll have something for tomorrow's rag, even if it's just to say that the authorities don't know anything. I'm sure little Leighton is working her fanny off trying to get something on this for A1, mostly the public panic angle, but I still get to be the guy who talks to the people with guns and badges.

"Big doings here," Sally Velez says.

"On a Sunday? I thought I had the only story in town today."

"This one's probably bigger to us than to the general public, although I'm sure the goddamn TV folks will be all over it, assuming they have anybody to do anything on a Sunday."

"What?"

"Sarah shot the fucker."

Yes, she really did it. Sally gives me the somewhat amusing details, although I doubt Luther Gates thinks they're so goddamn funny right now.

Gates apparently wasn't satisfied with just killing Sarah's dog and trying to kidnap her.

Still on the lam, he managed to get into the company parking garage this morning. The security cameras showed him slipping past the barrier shortly after nine, not long after the hard-working Sarah came in to begin another seventy-hour workweek.

Gates must have followed her there. The creep had to have been watching her house. Nothing else makes sense. You wouldn't assume that a sane person would come to work on Sunday morning after pulling a fourteen-hour shift the day before.

Sarah didn't stay in the office long. She reentered the parking garage about twelve thirty. That's when Luther Gates made his ill-conceived move.

"She said she saw something in her side-view mirror when she was getting ready to unlock the car. She said she wasn't sure at first that it was Gates, but she got her gun out of her purse anyhow."

Yeah, having somebody kill your dog and then try to carjack you will make you a bit more aware of your surroundings.

"She said that, by the time she could hear his footsteps, she had the gun out. When she turned around, there he was. She said he had a tire iron in his hand."

Never, ever bring a tire iron to a gunfight.

Sarah apparently shot him three times, once in his right arm, once in his left leg, and once in the nuts.

"He's going to live," Sally says, "but I don't think he's going to be much interested in going after young girls anytime soon. Not that there's going to be any, where he's going."

Sarah's actually a pretty good shot. I know from experience. She saved my bacon out on the Middle Peninsula back in 2016, and I doubt she's gotten worse in the interim. I almost always advise against civilians carrying loaded firearms, having seen the tragic consequences more than once. I've got to admit, though, Sarah did good.

"I doubt there's going to be any charges against her," Sally says.

* * *

I HEAD for the paper. Outside, between the front steps and Franklin Street, I see that some concrete barriers have been put in place. Too bad they didn't put some guards around the parking lot entrance earlier today.

It's kind of amusing to me that our publisher must think a daily newspaper is important enough to be blown up by nut cases. Well, Sarah can testify to the fact that we still have enough clout to piss some people off.

Wheelie's in the newsroom when I get there. I stop by and ask him if I can turn in the hours I spent as a guest of the Purifiers in that Scott's Addition warehouse as overtime.

He says he'll check into it.

"Think about all the life-insurance money I saved the Grimm Group by not getting my ass killed," I point out.

I stay in touch with the local, state, and federal law-enforcement folks the remainder of the day and night, but there isn't much to write beyond what we've said already: The Purifiers seem to have disappeared, and tomorrow's the sixteenth. Gird your loins.

There is one big near breakthrough though.

Late this afternoon, the feds thought they'd caught a break, but it didn't pan out. They were able to trace the Purity gang to an abandoned farm up in Hanover, based on that rare tip that actually bore fruit.

When they got there, though, all they found was a bunch of empty beer cans and fast-food wrappers, plus tire tracks that they could tie to one of the cars that was at the warehouse. Wherever the Purifiers were, they are still one step ahead of the law.

* * *

I GET in touch with Sarah at home. I congratulate her on her marksmanship.

"Well," she says, "I wasn't really trying to kill him, just maybe fuck him up a little."

Mission accomplished, I reply.

She says that she and Jack were planning to go out this afternoon to the animal shelter, to look for a replacement for Grover.

"Do you think they'll charge me with anything?"

I tell her that Sally doesn't think so. Neither do I. The tire iron Luther Gates was wielding probably entitled her to a few gratuitous shots with that Glock 43. Here in the Old Dominion, we're pretty sanguine about letting you shoot people who are trying to kidnap or kill you.

"You know," she says, "the only bad thing about this is that now I'm probably going to be the poster girl for the NRA. You know, 'It takes a good woman with a gun . . .' Hell, I've already gotten an e-mail from some gun-nut group."

I tell her that it could be an opportunity.

"You can point out that there's a not-so-fine line between carrying a gun for self-protection and trying to stop lunatics from buying rocket launchers."

"But then I won't be able to pick up big bucks shilling for the NRA," she says.

"Virtue has its price."

We tell each other that we're very glad that we are both still among the breathing. We tell each other to be careful. We both know how likely that is to happen.

When I check out after eleven P.M., we're still pretty sure something bad's going to happen tomorrow. Somewhere.

CHAPTER EIGHTEEN

Monday, September 16

I didn't sleep much last night. Cindy, who's taking a well-day off from school, stayed up with me until after two. Even after self-medicating with Early Times, I didn't fall off until sometime after three thirty.

She traced her finger along the various cuts and bruises I got courtesy of the Purifiers and tugged on my misshaped right ear, a souvenir of a bullet last year that made my sorry-ass life pass before my eyes briefly, and noted that perhaps I should consider a safer line of work, like crash-test dummy. She said she thought I had the brains for it.

* * *

AND THEN I'm awake at 6:05. I don't know what roused me, but something made me think about a farm I've never visited, up in Hanover County. Call it a hunch. Playing hunches isn't a very smart way to live your life, but hunches have sometimes led me where reason fears to tread.

Cindy wakes up long enough to ask me where the hell I'm going. I tell her I'll be back in a while, and not to worry.

"My ass," she says. "Wherever you're going, I'm going with you."

Nothing can stop an Oregon Hill girl when she makes up her mind.

"Should we be armed?" she asks as she follows me out the door, tucking her blouse into her jeans.

I tell her I don't think so.

"Don't think so?" she asks, obviously not finding that a satisfactory answer.

I amend my statement and tell her that we'll be safe, but that I'd be very happy if she'd go back and return her shapely ass to our nice, warm bed.

"I'm tired of worrying about whether I'm going to see you again, or just view you," she says. "If you gotta go, I'm going with you."

"What about Butterball? Who'll feed the cat?"

She advises me that, in the pecking order, I do rank above our fat feline. This is reassuring.

"By the way," she says, as we're walking out the Prestwould's front door and down the steps, "where are we going?"

When I tell her, she has another question:

"Why?"

I tell her I'm not sure, but I'll know pretty soon whether it's a wild-goose chase or not.

The sun is just peeking over the buildings downtown when we stumble out to the Honda.

We fight the rush-hour traffic on I-64 West, then exit onto 33 headed out of town, eventually crossing the Chickahominy into Hanover. We pass farms, abandoned stores, and Tea Party billboard screeds. I know the side road where we're supposed to turn, but not much else. I pull over and make L.D. Jones's day by calling him at home and interrupting his breakfast to get more specific directions.

If a farmhouse in Hanover County is the last place the Purifiers were seen, I'd like to take a look for myself.

L.D. tells me that the feds went over the farm with the proverbial fine-tooth comb and didn't find much of anything.

"But if you got nothing better to do, then knock yourself out."

The chief sounds tired. The fact that he's willing to let me set foot on anything resembling a crime scene emits more than a whiff of desperation. Today, one way or the other, is likely to be D-Day, and we're still flying blind.

I find the place, with the aid of the chief's directions and Cindy's navigational skills. As I'd been told, there's a county deputy and one Richmond cop there, keeping watch.

When we pull into the dirt driveway, I see that the city sent none other than my old pal Gillespie.

I honk my horn and make him slosh his coffee. He's munching on a Honey Bun and bullshitting with the young county cop.

"No donut shops out this way?" I inquire.

He grumbles but defers cursing when he sees that I have a comely female in tow.

"I've heard so much about you," Cindy says, which causes Gillespie to give me the fisheye.

I congratulate him on his astuteness in figuring out the significance of September 16 to Randall Heil. He is taken aback by my rare kindness toward him, once he figures out that I'm not being sarcastic.

"That donut shit is gettin' old," he growls when we're out of Cindy's earshot. I assure him that I meant no offense. Everybody, after all, loves a Sugar Shack donut. I don't say that some people just seem to love them more than others.

At any rate, Gillespie, who's gotten the word from the chief, assures the deputy that it's OK for me to snoop around the place.

"What the hell," he says as Cindy and I go inside. "If they haven't caught 'em yet . . ."

"Why are we here?" Cindy asks. "They're long gone from here, right?"

I explain that there might be something here that the feds missed. Something, anything. Time's almost out. What have we got to lose?

The place is pretty much of a wreck, greatly resembling the joint in Scott's Addition with its broken beer bottles and assorted trash. It looks like nobody's lived here for years.

I wander around, into the kitchen and bedrooms and the toilet that was used a time or three despite the fact that it probably was drained years ago.

"Gross," Cindy observes.

I walk around back, almost falling through the rotting porch. In some places, whole sections of wood have fallen into the dirt below.

I glance down into the dark, and I see something, barely visible.

By kicking a few more boards loose, I make a hole wide enough that I can ease my way through. When Cindy, who's been walking around the backyard, comes up, the remaining porch floor is at my waist level.

I reach down and am able to grab what I saw—a yellow legal pad that missed the attention of the feds. And now I think I know why we're here.

Bug, the crazy little fucker who pitched my cell phone and "directed" me to the warehouse, was a doodler. I could see him there in the background, behind Randall Heil and his other henchmen, while I wondered if that was the last room I'd ever see. He was drawing on a notepad—a yellow legal pad. For a terrorist, he did seem a little buggy.

We used to have an editor who did that. He said it helped him survive the interminable and meaningless meetings that comprised most of his day.

Bug, it appears, is similarly inclined. Maybe he pitched it when the Purifiers left in a hurry. Maybe he figured slipping it through that hole in the back porch was as good a plan as any. Before my misstep, the hole wasn't all that big.

I extricate myself back onto the porch with Cindy's help, then take the legal pad, not much worse for wear since the porch is still covered by what passes for a roof, and walk over to one of the rusted-out lawn chairs.

Flipping through the pad, I find sketches of people and weird-ass diagrams and, of course, the expected Nazi and Confederate symbols. Some of the drawings of women make Cindy go "eww." We agree that Bug's future as an artist was limited at best.

There's nothing on the pad that gives me any clue about what the Purifiers are targeting. Maybe the FBI geniuses, who somehow missed this yesterday, can find meaning here.

But then I flip to the last page on which Bug was practicing his craft.

I look at it. Cindy, who's standing behind me, leans over my shoulder.

"Is that what I think it is?" she asks.

"If it isn't, I don't know what the hell else it could be."

I walk around the house.

"What you got there?" Gillespie asks, brushing crumbs off his uniform.

I tell him that it appears he is not the only Richmonder who's in line for a junior detective merit badge.

CHAPTER NINETEEN

"The fucking Rotunda? Are you shitting me?"

No, I explain to the chief. For real.

He's in the makeshift operations room with the rest of the terrorism brain trust, hoping for a miracle and waiting for the worst.

I explain to L.D., who puts me on speakerphone, about the drawing.

"You're sure it's the Rotunda?"

It's pretty damn hard to mistake it for something else, I tell him. When Thomas Jefferson had the thing built as the centerpiece of his new University of Virginia almost two hundred years ago, he meant for it to attract attention. Cindy tells me it's a World Heritage Site, which sounds impressive.

Whatever it is, it apparently seemed like a fine spot for Randall Heil and his merry band to make something go boom.

And I'm not just conjecturing about the "boom" part. In Bug's artwork, above the Rotunda is a cartoonish starburst radiating outward and, honest to God, the word "boom" with an exclamation point.

The feds are here in twenty minutes.

They seem to take the drawing seriously. When I suggest that maybe some sharp-eyed G-man might have spotted that notepad in the dirt below the back porch, they are noncommittal.

"Doesn't say when," one of them mutters.

Since we're pretty sure it's sometime today, I suggest that it might be a good idea if somebody, local, state, or federal, made a quick run up to Charlottesville before the pride and joy of the University of Virginia, along with a bunch of students and faculty, gets blown to smithereens. We're more than eight hours into what seems like a day that could live in infamy.

"We're already on it," I am assured.

I get back in the Honda.

"Where are we going?" my beloved asks.

"You're going back to the Prestwould," I inform her.

"Not fucking likely," she informs me. "You get to have all the fun. I know you're headed to Charlottesville, and I'm going with you."

It does no good to explain that people are very likely to get hurt or killed before this whole mess is over.

She reiterates that she is not budging.

"Well, if you're going to be so damn bullheaded, the least you can do is drive."

So she takes the wheel. It's a little over an hour to C'ville from the farm, time for me to make the newsroom aware of the latest developments.

I call Sarah, because I knew she'd be there bright and early, not one to let a little thing like yesterday's shooting keep her away.

"Good news," she says before I can tell her anything. "They're not going to charge me."

"Well, they shouldn't."

"My thoughts exactly, although the police did give me a stern warning about going around shooting people."

"Unless they deserve to be shot."

"They seemed to want to reserve the needs-to-be-shot option for trained professionals."

"Yeah," I say, "I understand. It's like if some civilian tried to tell you he could run a newsroom better than you."

"Not a good analogy. They do that all the time anyhow."

Luther Gates will live, I'm told, but it might not be a very happy life.

"So," Sarah says, "were you just calling to see how I was doing?"

I inform her that this is not the case.

"Holy fucking shit," our assistant managing editor says. "The Rotunda? How dare they?"

Sarah is a University of Virginia graduate, and she seems to take special umbrage at the Purifiers' choice of target.

I explain that it isn't a certainty, but based on what I've found, it seems extremely likely.

She says she'll dispatch a photographer.

"And I assume you're on the way too."

"Already a few miles from the Gum Spring exit. We'll be there in forty-five minutes."

She asks me if I have any idea when the big bang might occur.

No, I explain. We just figure it's sometime today.

"The Rotunda," Sarah repeats. "I'd like to shoot those bastards."

I note that maybe she's done enough shooting for one week.

"I only shoot the guilty," she says.

By the time we get to the exit for the U.Va. campus, it's after nine. I've talked with L.D. once already. He beat us there by about ten minutes.

"It's a clusterfuck up here, Willie," he says. "I don't know if you're going to be able to get in. But they're pretty sure they've found something."

The chief is right. I can't drive any closer to the Rotunda than the parking garage on Emmett Street. It's about a quarter of a mile away, uphill all the way. Cindy says she doesn't think I'm allowed to smoke on the campus, or the Grounds as they say up here. While lighting up, I tell her that I think the authorities have bigger issues today than me and my Camels.

It takes a while to get close to the scene. I have to talk my way past all kinds of law enforcement folks, most of whom don't seem to take my Virginia Press Association card very seriously.

Finally, though, closing on ten o'clock, we are able to make our way to University Avenue, with the Rotunda looming over us to our right. Ahead, a little ways up the hill, I see a cluster of people in law-enforcement uniforms and suits. They are looking toward the Rotunda. More specifically, they seem to be attracted to a vehicle of some kind, parked in the shadow of the building, maybe three hundred yards away.

It is some kind of truck, like the kind you see maintenance crews use to keep college campuses looking so good that nobody minds going into eternal debt just to attend classes there. Whoever drove it up there must have used the brick pathway the truck sits beside.

Once we're able to sneak and cajole our way into the general vicinity of the cops, I find L.D., who has no jurisdiction here but understandably felt like he should be at the scene anyhow.

"They say somebody left the truck there overnight," he says, not turning away from it. I notice that we're standing close to a poplar tree so big that, if something goes boom, maybe we can duck behind it and save ourselves. Or it'll fall on us. "Nobody saw anybody move it there. It was just there this morning. Nobody knows whose it is. It doesn't belong to the university."

I move in front of Cindy, as if that'd help.

What the authorities do know is that the truck isn't carrying a load of mulch.

What it seems to be packed with, the chief tells me, is ammonium nitrate, aka fertilizer, along with some other stuff that, when it all goes off, is likely to leave a big-ass crater right where the Rotunda won't be standing anymore.

"It's like what that McVeigh asshole did in Oklahoma City," L.D. says. "And from what the feds tell me, it's just about that big."

I instinctively start edging back a bit, pulling Cindy with me.

"So what are they doing about it?"

It turns out that there's one very brave son of a bitch from some federal agency who's trying to disarm it before he and everything around him is atomized.

I can see him up there. He's the only one close to the truck. All the faculty and staff anywhere near the Rotunda have been scrambled, along with a goodly number of students, a few hundred of whom are standing maybe one hundred yards in back of us, between us and the bars and joints along the street below.

The crowd seems more giddy than uneasy, confident as only the young can be that nothing bad could possibly happen to them or their beloved campus.

"Do they know what time the thing's supposed to go off?" I ask.

"They said it was set to go at five minutes until eleven."

Yeah, that'd be about right, if you were going for maximum death and destruction. Lots of students and faculty pouring out, between classes.

"Bastards," Cindy observes.

I don't think the students know the timetable. If they do, they aren't terribly concerned. The cops are having a hell of a time keeping them at least marginally out of harm's way.

I look at my watch: 10:46.

"C'mon, man," I hear the chief mutter.

And then, when I look up, the guy is rising from the underside of the truck. He gives the thumbs-up.

A big roar arises from the students behind us, who'll maybe think more kindly of people with badges, for the next day or two at least.

An impressive array of media folk has gotten word of our little drama. By the time I work my way through the advancing students and get to the base of the Rotunda steps, there are at least half a dozen TV camera crews here, plus several still photographers. I see our guy Chip Grooms, among them. There are reporters from all the TV stations and the local paper plus the *Washington Post* guy who's their one-man Richmond bureau.

Nothing like a dramatic news story with a happy ending, except maybe one with an unhappy ending.

The FBI's lead guy is holding forth in front of the Rotunda, five steps from the bottom. In typically gracious federal employee fashion, he says the bureau got a lead this morning from a source and closed in quickly to save the day. He doesn't mention, *quelle surprise!*, that the tip came from a tired-ass newspaper reporter who found something the G-men had overlooked.

Somebody asks if they know who the perpetrators are.

This leads to a groan or two from the idiot's compatriots. Anybody with a working brain knows Purity has been planning this little fireworks display, had already taken credit for it prematurely, as a matter of fact.

I ask a question.

"Have Randall Heil or any of the Purifiers been apprehended?"

The fed frowns.

"We are working on that right now. I can't talk about it, because it's . . ."

". . . an ongoing investigation." I complete the sentence for him. He does not seem appreciative.

Well, the sun is shining, nobody died, and the Rotunda is still standing. Not a bad day, considering the alternative.

But those guys are still out there.

A student has just returned to stand outside his room on the Lawn, where they let the really smart kids live in nineteenth-century squalor. I ask him if I can borrow the chair that's next to him.

He's accommodating. I file what I can for our online readers while he gives Cindy a tour of his modest dwelling.

"Were they really going to blow up the Rotunda?" he asks when they come out.

"That was the plan," I tell him.

"Man," he says, "why didn't they stop those guys sooner? We could've been killed."

It probably does no good, but I do point out to him that his glass is a good bit more than half full this fine day.

My biggest coup probably is getting an interview with the guy who actually defused the bomb. The chief fed, who does not seem to really like me much, pulls me aside and asks if I'd like to talk to the guy. Solo.

"Our way of saying, 'thank you'," he says, leaving me uncharacteristically speechless.

The guy, who's with Homeland Security, is maybe ten years older than the college kids watching the drama unfold like it was a damn football game. He is a tad on the laconic side. You'd expect that of someone who makes a living doing something that gets yourself and a lot of other people killed if you do it wrong. He probably has a pulse rate of forty.

"How big a hole would it have made if that thing had gone off?" I ask.

"Oh," he says, "if it'd exploded, there'd probably be eighteenth-century bricks raining all over Charlottesville."

He estimates that the crater would have been about fifty feet deep, "but that's just an estimate."

I have to ask:

"Don't you get nervous, doing what you do?"

He frowns at me.

"Nervous? Hell, no. What's to be nervous about? If I screw up, I won't be alive long enough to suffer."

He says he's already done two tours of Iraq. He's seen a bomb or two.

"When one of these things does go off, it can mess up our whole damn day."

As Cindy and I are getting ready to hoof it back to Richmond so I can start filling up some column inches for tomorrow's paper, I see L.D. among the law enforcement types. He and they look more animated than they should, I think. I see several of them talking on their cell phones and moving rather briskly.

"What is it?" I ask the chief.

He stops for a moment, considering the downside of telling a nosy-ass reporter anything.

"They think they've got a bead on them," he says.

I ask for details.

"Some farmer, over at the store at Zion Crossroads, called the cops and said he'd seen a couple of guys who looked like the description of the Purifiers, turning down a county road just south of there off US 250.

Holy shit. The coincidence is too great to be a coincidence.

"L.D.," I say, "would you like to know where exactly those bastards are right now?"

I was all set to take Cindy to the Riverside for the best burgers in the state of Virginia. I tell her she's going to have to wait.

"Quit your bitching," I advise. "You were the one who insisted on coming with me."

CHAPTER TWENTY

"Do the math," I tell L.D.

The crumbling estate that the late Whitney Charles owned is no more than three miles from Zion Crossroads, where some sharp-eyed farmer thinks he saw some of the Purifiers. They knew where the house was, according to Randall Heil. They knew, duh, that nobody was living there at present.

The chief concedes that there's at least an even chance that I'm right in pinpointing the whereabouts of Heil and the other Purifiers.

It doesn't take long for L.D. to spread the word to the various state and federal folks still sucking each other's dicks over preventing massive carnage and architectural desecration.

The chief came up here to Charlottesville by himself. He reluctantly agrees to let Cindy and me ride with him out to Whit Charles's place. I figure we'll have a better chance of getting close to the action if we're in the company of the Richmond police chief.

"Don't get used to this," L.D. says. "It's not like you're my goddamn buddy or something."

He apologizes to Cindy for the foul language.

"Jesus, L.D.," she says, "I'm married to a journalist."

By the time we get there, it's a three-ring circus.

The place is just across the Louisa County line. The feds have already determined that at least one of the cars they can see from their vantage point a quarter of a mile away matches one that was part of the Purity entourage last Friday night.

The state police, ever on the cutting edge of technology, have deployed a drone to survey the property from a safe distance, and it's been determined that a couple of guys who seem to be packing shit into a van match the descriptions of two of the Purifiers.

"We figure by now they know that their little plan has backfired," a state cop tells me. "It looks like they're getting ready to clear out, or at least they were."

Yeah, if we can see them, they can see us.

But apparently they didn't act fast enough once they discovered that their bomb didn't go off. As far as I can see, there's only one way out of the late Whit Charles's place, and we're right in the middle of it.

I don't know if the state guy knows I'm a working journalist or not, but I'm not disabusing him. Hitching a ride with L.D. is looking like a smooth move, since the authorities have shut off all traffic a mile back on the humpbacked country road leading here.

In the aftermath of 9/11, it seems like every law-enforcement entity in the United States has been gifted with the kind of high-tech shit that gives civil libertarians nightmares. It can come in handy though. If the good guys don't win this one, it won't be because they don't have enough firepower. I see all kinds of war-worthy rifles and grenade launchers being set up. There are plenty of mean-looking guys with body armor that would have stood them well in Iraq or Afghanistan. Don't know how they got here so goddamn fast.

A little after two in the afternoon, the good guys are ready to make their move.

"Here we go," says L.D. He directs Cindy and me to get behind one of the monster vehicles that have been rolling in here over the last hour.

Some kind of armored monstrosity is making its way across the open field facing the house, chewing up the red clay with its treads. L.D. says he thinks it belongs to the National Guard. There are a half-dozen heavily armed men jogging along behind it, using it for cover.

The chief looks like he'd like to have one of those big-boy toys for his own cops.

This thing, which looks like a tank, stops maybe half-way between us and the house.

And then the loudspeakers kick in.

"Randall Heil," the voice booms out across the countryside, "we know you're in there. Come out and nobody will get hurt."

The message is repeated a couple more times. And then, having given the bad guys warning enough, the tank is ordered to move forward.

A few seconds later, we hear gunfire. We assume it came from the house, because we can see the six guys behind the armored vehicle, and I can't argue with the subsequent claims by the feds that they were fired on first.

However it happened, the guys in the armored vests return fire with a vengeance. Having never served in the military, I never really had an appreciation of the firepower of your basic assault rifle until a couple of rounds fired from Whit Charles's house hit the side of the truck we were crouched behind. They sounded as if they would have ruined somebody's day if they had hit flesh instead of metal.

I am not so eager to watch the proceedings after that, only peeking out whenever the firing ceases for a few seconds.

"If you wait to hear a shot before you duck," L.D. advises, "you'll be dead before you hear it."

I think I knew that.

The fireworks go on for another ten minutes. And then another behemoth comes rolling down the hill toward the house.

By this time, we've learned that one of the FBI guys has been hit. They're not sure what's going on in the house, having gotten nothing from their demand to surrender except the proverbial hail of gunfire.

The guy on the loudspeaker again offers to let the Purifiers come out, promising no harm.

By this time, though, I can kind of figure where this is going for Purity: South.

They've wounded, if not killed, a federal agent. The cops don't know how many people are holed up in the house, which is now a bit worse for wear after being used as target practice by guys with military-grade firepower. To the best of their knowledge, though, there are no women or children inside, so there is not an overload of concern about whether the Purifiers come out hands up or feet first.

In other words, it won't look like Waco. Killing these fuckers won't be a PR disaster for anybody.

And making an unhappy ending even more likely for them is this: They know, if they have brains, that they are in such deep shit by now that many of them will die in prison once they surrender.

So one side has the green light and the other has nothing to lose.

The lead vehicle gets even closer, and then I start hearing these loud explosions, louder than the gunfire.

"Grenade launchers," says L.D.

And then I can see flames coming from the roof on one side of the house. Then you can see fire through one of the windows.

We keep waiting for somebody or somebodies to come out the front door, but nothing happens. Then I hear a voice over one of the radios saying something about "going around back."

Behind Whit Charles's house, it turns out, there's a marshy area leading to a big creek, a tributary of the South Anna. While we were holed up behind a truck watching the frontal assault, the FBI had a few of its men loop around behind the house, wisely deducing that the place also had a back door.

We hear another burst of gunfire, now coming from farther away.

"They're running," I hear over the radio.

Apparently most of the Purifiers were gunned down as they tried to either make their last stand or head for the creek.

Randall Heil didn't go down easy.

He got as far as the creek, was in the middle of it, according to the agent I talk with later.

"And then we cut him in half," he says.

I ask if he was firing back.

"I'm pretty sure he was," the guy says. "Or at least he was about to. He definitely was thinking about it."

Close enough, as far as I'm concerned.

It takes another hour to patch the story together, based on what I can glean from the feds, state cops, and L.D. By the time the chief gives us a ride back to our car in Charlottesville, the sun is almost down behind the Blue Ridge, turning everything purple and gold.

Cindy says she's starving.

I call the newsroom and tell Sarah what's transpired. She knows some of the story already, but nobody but yours truly was within a country mile of the Purifiers' last stand.

"When can you write it?" she asks.

I tell her that I'll put something on the website in forty-five minutes and then send the rest later.

I sit on the concrete curb in the university parking garage beside the Honda and write something for the Internet freeloaders. Cindy has found a vending machine and brought us some Nabs and Cokes.

"Willie," she says, "I don't think I can make it back to Richmond without something other than goddamn crackers in my stomach."

The tendency is to tell her, again, that she volunteered—nay, insisted—on going on this little adventure.

But, fuck it, I'm starving too.

And so I produce the first draft of this little tidbit of history for our print readers sitting at a table at the Riverside, intermittently writing and munching down on the state's best hamburger.

CHAPTER TWENTY-ONE

Tuesday, September 17

By the time they finished the body count, they determined that there were nine Purifiers, including several that weren't present for my warehouse ordeal.

And, yes, the past tense is appropriate for each and every one of the bastards. They found five bodies in the house. Two died from gunfire or grenades. Three apparently succumbed to smoke inhalation.

Three others met Jesus trying to get to the creek, before the feds bagged Randall Heil himself.

The good news, at the end of the day: two law enforcement agents wounded, but expected to survive, and nine Purifiers gone to their reward.

Chip Grooms, our photographer, wasn't able to get within a mile of the place, but I did get a few pretty passable shots with my iPhone camera.

"Not bad for an amateur," Grooms grumped.

I reminded him that they probably were better than the pictures he was taking of his dick while standing behind the police barricade halfway back to Charlottesville.

After I dropped Cindy off at the Prestwould, I reported to the word factory and started spilling my guts for the print edition.

Sally Velez says I might have set the record for most trees killed in one day in pursuit of journalism.

First, I had to tell our breathless readers about how a clue found underneath a porch in Hanover County by an enterprising reporter led to a last-minute reprieve for the Rotunda. I also had a nifty sidebar on the Homeland Security guy who actually defused the bomb. So far, I have not heard anything from our genius publisher about letting Leighton Byrd interview me and write the story herself, seeing as how I'm too close to it.

Most of our audience already knew a lot of the details of the University of Virginia drama, since it made both the local and national news last night. The stuff about my finding the drawing, though, was new to them. It was new to the other news outlets too. I know because the *Post*, the AP, and the *New York Times* have already left me messages wanting to interview me about it. I guess, in the aftermath of all the Neo-Nazi unpleasantness in Charlottesville back in 2017, a report of skinheads almost succeeding in blowing up the Rotunda did have some legs to it.

Hell, if I'm not going to let little Leighton interview me for my own rag, I'm sure as hell not going to give my stuff away to other newspapers.

The story I really had by the short hairs, though, was the one on what took place out at the late Whit Charles's place in Louisa County. Of course, the AP and everybody else had the basics. A couple of TV news crews even got shots from helicopters of the carnage as the house went up in flames and the Purifiers scattered and met their well-deserved fates.

But they weren't on the ground.

You spend a lifetime in this business hoping to be the one reporter there when national-level news breaks out. And this was it.

"When the smoke cleared and the bodies had all been accounted for," my story opened, "the charred remnants of a Confederate battle flag drooped from the wall of the burned-out house where nine hate-mongers made their pathetic last stand."

"Isn't that editorializing a little bit?" Wheelie asked as he looked over my shoulder.

I gave him, chapter and verse, the reasons why I felt I was well within the boundaries of truth in calling Randall Heil and his minions hate-mongers and calling their self-destructive denouement pathetic.

He said he guessed I was right.

I also did an interview with the chief fed, who went into great detail about how hard the FBI tried to reach a peaceful settlement but, in the end, had no choice. Wink, wink.

And there was a sidebar on the nine dead Purifiers. Leighton did get to write that one, with information she got from the feds. It irks me that we give scum like that a bit of posthumous exposure. Will a nerdy kid who can't get laid read it and think that these guys are heroes? That's what we do though.

In the end, it wasn't a bad day's work.

Wheelie said he'd see about me getting some overtime.

* * *

CINDY'S HEADED back to school today. Young minds are waiting to be stuffed with knowledge.

Since yesterday was supposed to be a "sick" day, I peered up at her from our bed and asked how she was going to explain to her students and coworkers her little sojourn to Charlottesville on a day when she was supposed to be ailing.

"Hell," she said as she was fishing for her keys, "who's going to tell them? You?"

I remind her of something. When we were leaving the carnage scene in Louisa County yesterday in the police chief's car, with me in the front with L.D. and her in the back, an enterprising reporter from one of the Richmond stations managed to flag down the chief and ask him a couple of questions. L.D. didn't really tell the guy anything, but the cameraman with him did get a good shot of us all, including the lady in the back seat.

"I saw it on the late news last night," I tell her, "and I'm sure it'll be on again today. Your hair looked good."

"Damn," my beloved said. "Busted."

* * *

The cat and I tolerate each other while I ease into my day with some dry cereal and a couple of cups of coffee. Night cops doesn't start until midafternoon, but there are more stories to write.

On the way out, I run into Clara Westbrook, my favorite octogenarian Prestwouldian, in the lobby.

Clara, bless her heart, still has a print newspaper delivered to her door every morning. She's pulling her little oxygen buddy behind her, waiting for somebody to drive her somewhere.

"Willie," she says, "you had quite the day yesterday, it seems."

I agree that yesterday was one for the books.

"Don't you think you're getting a little old for this kind of tomfoolery? I mean, don't they have some young people at the paper?"

Yeah, I concede, they do. And as soon as the suits decide that I'm past due date and start sending Leighton Byrd and her peers out to cover the good stuff, my days in the newsroom are numbered. Youth works cheap.

"Yes," Clara says, "I guess you're right. I've been our church historian for thirty-eight years, and sometimes it just seems too much to keep up with. But if I let them know that, they won't think I'm young anymore."

We laugh, and it occurs to me that this is the first time I've done that lately.

* * *

WHEN I get to the newsroom, ten-ish, we're already in "what have you done for me lately?" mode.

There is need for an all-encompassing thumb-sucker. There are so many loose ends to tie up.

I call Marcus Green to find out what's happening with Jerome Sheets, now that he's not headed for life or worse as a murderer.

Marcus tells me that the kid is actually out on bail.

"His momma came up with the money somehow," he says. Marcus and I both are pretty sure that young Jerome owes his at least temporary freedom to the largesse of Big Boy Sunday.

"Did Big Boy pay you too?" I ask.

"Oh, yes," Marcus says. "He paid me very well. And he'll pay me even better if I can get the boy off with probation."

I wish him luck. Maybe a few days in the city jail will be enough to convince Big Boy's charge and likely offspring to be, if not more law-abiding, at least more careful. If he's going to hang out with Big Boy Sunday, careful is about the best we can hope for.

I get Jerome's mom's number, but neither she nor her son have anything printable to say for public consumption.

I also give a call to George "Snake" Davis, Stick's brother. I haven't talked with him since the memorial service. I thought he might have a few words about how this has all played out.

"So he got his ass killed because he was messing around with a bunch of damn Nazis?"

I explain that they were neo-Nazis.

"What's the damn difference?" Snake asks.

"Not much," I concede, except that the latter don't at present have the right to fulfill their fantasies.

I go on to stress that I don't really believe that Stick bought into all that crap, and that he seems to have been trying to help bring them to justice.

"Well, damn," his brother says, "he ought to have just left that to the cops."

He gives me a passable and maybe even sincere quote about missing Stick. But he has one more question before I hang up:

"Is there any reward?"

"Reward?"

"You know. Like would Stick have been in line for some kind of reward of some kind, for helping to stop those assholes?"

I see where this is going.

I tell Snake that I don't think there is a reward, and I don't think rewards get passed along to the next of kin, but that I'll let him know if I find out anything.

"Well, shit," Snake says as I hang up.

Terri McAllister actually calls me.

"That was some story," she says. "Who knew ol' Stick had such a backstory? I wish he'd have told me what he was up to. Of course, if he had, they might have come after me. Sometimes silence is golden, you know?"

She confesses to "kind of missing" Stick. After she hangs up, it occurs to me that it's possible that the late Whit Charles gave more of a damn about Randolph Giles "Stick" Davis than either his only living kin or his last girlfriend.

Considering that Stick stole a considerable amount of money from Charles, that says something, although I'm damned if I know what.

I also got a tip from the feds, although I've got to put this one in my back pocket until everybody's hash is settled. In the weeds back of Whit Charles's house, along the path Randall Heil took en route to his reward, they found an iPad, apparently belonging to Heil. Miraculously the iPad had not been sufficiently damaged to keep the FBI guys from gleaning a few names off it.

The way I understand it, there will be quite a few arrests on charges related to attempted terrorism and various other things, over several states. Yesterday's shootout apparently did not completely rid us of Purifiers. I'm sure the impending busts won't either, but you've got to start somewhere. Keeping a lid on these assholes is like mowing the grass. You get everything looking nice and pretty, and before you know it, the weeds are popping up again.

Sarah stops by. She congratulates me for still being alive. I congratulate her for getting away with shooting a man and not getting charged with anything.

"Wheelie wants me to write something about it, a first-person account of being stalked. But I don't know, I haven't written anything for a while except goddamn memos and budgets."

I suggest that she could let Leighton interview her.

She snorts and says that will happen right after pigs grow wings.

⁂ ⁂ ⁂

THERE IS something else I want to write in addition to the big-picture piece.

It might take more than a day to do this one.

Stick Davis did not earn a lot of laurels in his foreshortened existence. He was careless, selfish, larcenous, and somewhat short of Einstein, brain-wise.

But what if he was trying to do one good deed in his sorry-ass life? What if he really was planning to pull the plug on the Purifiers after shaking them down and then making a bundle telling the whole story in his memoirs?

I point out to Wheelie and Sarah that without Stick, things could have gone very, very bad. He infiltrated Purity, got his hands on that video, and left enough hints for me to find the damn thing.

"Well," Wheelie says, "if he had that DVD, why didn't he just take it to the cops?"

Because he thought he was a player, I explain. He thought he could con everybody and still wind up saving the day.

CHAPTER TWENTY-TWO

Sunday, September 22

Who killed Stick Davis?

Maybe it's a moot point now, although L.D. Jones and his crack police force would like to clear it off the books, I'm sure.

It's a safe bet that the killer or killers were among the nine miscreants who died last Monday at Whit Charles's house in Louisa County. Randall Heil said as much, and a fifth-grader could've figured it out even without that. Maybe DNA or other cop magic will tell us who specifically did the deed.

The commonwealth's attorney must be relieved. No living perps means no trials.

The murders of Charles and his buddy Gino are equally solvable. Their killers are six feet under or at least on an autopsy table. Heil didn't make much effort to hide the Purifiers' role in the carnage.

Elsewhere the courts will be settling the hash of a few Purifiers for quite some time. The busts that went on all week put a dozen suspected terrorists in jails around the country. Randall Heil kept very good records of who his associates were, and they were from all over. California.

Idaho. Texas. Oregon. Indiana. For a resident of the former capital of the Confederacy, there is always guilty pleasure in seeing that all the racist Neanderthals don't live in the South.

* * *

As for Stick's mindset and motive, I have a better idea than I did a few days ago.

I went back and reread the half a manuscript I'd finished before I was deprived of the rest of my fifty-thousand-dollar fee and my subject was deprived of his life.

It's no fun reading what you've already written, and it can be a fool's errand. You never catch your own mistakes, and you're not excited about going back over what you already know. God bless copy editors.

Going back over Stick's memoirs, though, I remembered something.

In all the shitstorm that followed my finding Stick's body, I had forgotten about something he told me. It didn't seem pertinent to anything I'd written so far, but I wrote it down anyhow.

When he was talking about his life down in the islands one night, he digressed. He said something that he might have later told me to remove from the memoir, if we'd gotten that far.

"Something big is coming," he said, according to my hen-scratch notes. "When it happens, a lot of people are going to be surprised. They might start having a different perspective on Randolph Giles Davis. They might think he wasn't such a bad dude after all."

He referred to himself in the third person a lot.

At the time, I thought it was just Stick being a gasbag. But, neurotic note-taker that I am, I wrote it down anyhow.

Stick was often about as clear as an Afton Mountain fogbank. There was always the feeling, as the project plodded along, that my old drinking partner was jerking my chain a little. But, hell, the first check hadn't bounced.

I remember asking him if he could give me a little more to work with than that throwaway comment, such as what the fuck "something" was.

"In good time," I remember him saying, blowing a smoke ring and winking. I left it at that.

So I am left to conjecture. If he had just said something big was going to happen, I'd have written him off as a careless, thoughtless bastard who was willing to play games with people's lives.

But he said that what happened might make the world think he wasn't the complete broke-dick that logic told us he was.

And it jibes with what the late Whit Charles said when he was filling me in on Stick's island days.

Having been given the benefit of the doubt on many occasions, I am willing to repackage one of those gifts and cut Stick Davis some slack.

Maybe he was trying to play both ends against the middle, playing footsy with some bad dudes but still planning to rain on their fireworks before things went too far. And getting a nice book deal out of it.

To plagiarize what little I remember of Shakespeare, it's possible Stick was trying to do a good deed in a naughty world.

At any rate, that's what I'm telling our shrinking readership in the appallingly subjective piece that ran on A1 this morning. If Stick wasn't a hero, I'd like our readers to believe he wanted to be one.

❋ ❋ ❋

The crowd at Joe's back table this morning is larger than usual, to the delight of our server. R.P. and Brooklyn are there, along with Cindy and me, Abe and Stella Stellar, Andy Peroni and his missus, and, all the way from Ohio, Francis Xavier "Goat" Johnson.

"Man," Goat said as he sucked down his second cheap Bloody Mary, "you've got more lives than a cat."

Everybody wants to talk about Stick Davis. They've all read this morning's story. The ones who knew him tend to pooh-pooh the idea that the Stickster had it in him to do something heroic.

I point out that, without him, the Rotunda would be but a fond memory, and that the University of Virginia would be without some of its best and brightest.

"Yeah," Andy said, "but he had to get his ass killed for that to happen, and except for him saying that he was going to do something that might make people reconsider his status as an asshole, we don't know that he wasn't the same old Stick."

"Aw, nobody's all bad," R.P. put in. "I remember one time, back probably thirty-five years ago, him and me were at the 7-Eleven, at the checkout, and I was buying a case of Old Milwaukee. I was like half a dollar short. And Stick, who didn't even know me except through Willie, covered me."

We are all silent for a few seconds.

Finally, Stella, fresh off her tour of Virginia's hinterlands, says, "Goddamn. That's the best you can come up with? This guy really was an asshole."

"Well," I chip in when the laughter subsides, "I never caught him cheating at poker."

"If he ever knocked a girl up," said Andy, "I never heard about it."

"Damn," Stella says, "I can't believe his ass hasn't been nominated for sainthood."

In the end, we'll all agree that, when it comes to Stick Davis, we should try to believe the best and, if not speak kindly of the dead, at least not speak ill.

* * *

I've decided, with the blessing of almost no one at the paper, to do my best to finish, or at least rewrite, Stick's autobiography. It'll be a challenge, for a guy who is used to writing what needs to be written in a hurry and then moving on to the next homicide. But, what the hell, I've got half a book already. And maybe somebody will pay me to finish it, now that Stick has achieved at least temporary notoriety.

Hell, I could use the money, since the Chipster continues to try to wheedle his mom into investing a chunk of her nest egg in his future as a restaurateur. Maybe someday we'll find out what Stick did with the rest of the money he stole from Whit Charles.

Since Stick himself is not around to tell us how he intended for his story to end, I'll have to switch to the third person, my preference as a habitual journalist anyway. And Stick won't be looking over my shoulder on this one. At least, I hope not.

Benson Stine, our publisher, does not want me wasting valuable time when I could be covering double homicides instead of writing a book. When I gave him the option of dropping the subject or turning in the boatload of overtime I've meticulously logged while covering this whole affair, his objections seem to drift away like dust in the wind.

"Well," he said after we talked about it, rather loudly, in his office the other day, "just be sure you give the paper the full forty hours we pay you for."

I told him that if I cut my workweek short at forty hours, somebody else would have to cover Saturday night's felonious festivities in our fair city.

Sally Velez and Wheelie just think I'm pissing in the wind.

"Who's going to give a shit about a guy like that?" Sally inquires.

Wheelie wonders how I'm going to make it work, since nobody really knows what was in Stick Davis's mind toward the end.

Sarah, bless her heart, told me to go for it.

"Hell," she said, "half the quote-unquote nonfiction stuff I read has a big dollop of bullshit in it. Write what he said and then write what you think he meant, and you'll be all right. You'll be his interpreter."

She also says that she and Jack are definitely getting another dog.

"With that fucking Gates in jail for, I hope, the rest of his natural life, our next pup ought to be safe."

I mention that perhaps she should get a cat instead. You don't have to walk them, and they've made great strides with litter boxes.

I tell her I know where she can get one for free.

* * *

I make what probably won't be my last trip to Westwood.

The landlord let Terri McAllister and me come over and make a pass at whatever Stick left behind. Snake said he couldn't care less about it unless we found some money there.

It was a furnished apartment, so it's mostly clothes and books that are left. I take any papers I can find that seem even remotely relevant to the book, since I don't have the notebooks. Terri wants one of his flannel shirts, one I'd seen him wear many times.

She holds it up to her face.

"Still smells like him," she says. Tough broad that she is, I think she might be on the verge of a tear or two.

When we're leaving and the landlord is locking up behind me, I see a familiar face scowling at us one house down.

Mrs. Woolfolk doesn't remember me at first, maybe thinks I'm just another cop digging into the murder next door. When I jog her memory, she lets down her guard a bit.

"Yes, I remember you," she says. "My goodness, that was some story. You never know about folks. He seemed like such a nice man. Well, maybe not so much nice but, you know, harmless."

I reiterate what I've written in the paper. It's possible Stick meant well.

"Could be," she says. "One good thing came out of it, though, other than not having the Rotunda turned into a brick pile."

"What's that?"

"Folks are talking about Jordan's Branch again. The younger ones, the ones whose parents moved out to the suburbs long ago, they didn't even know about it."

It turns out that there's a move afoot now to get the city to bring Jordan's Branch back to the surface again, which I guess would require having water running down the median strip of Staples Mill Road.

"A lot of folks were baptized there," Mrs. Woolfolk says. "It had a lot of meaning in the black community. And back in the day, before the city graced us with the city services we were paying taxes for, there was a spring there where people got their water. We've been talking to our councilman about turning it into a real creek again."

She waves to a neighbor.

"They say they don't know what they might find if they start trying to bring that creek back to life. Might be anything down there."

I wish Mrs. Woolfolk all the luck in the world. Hell, it wouldn't be the worst use of city funds I've seen. If I weren't an unbiased journalist, I'd sign a petition to get it done.

* * *

I LIGHT a Camel and think of Mrs. Woolfolk and Jordan's Branch.

She's right. You don't know what you'll find when you start digging.